"Carina Bissett is one of my favorite speculative authors writing today—magic and myth, horror and revenge, wonder and hope. Her stories are original, lyrical, and haunting—Shirley Jackson mixed with Ursula LeGuin and a dash of Neil Gaiman. An amazing collection of stories." —Richard Thomas, author of *Spontaneous Human Combustion*, a Bram Stoker Award finalist

"Carina Bissett's collection is a thing of wonder and beauty. It is a true representation of Carina herself: whimsical, visceral, lovely, and fierce. You can hear women's voices screaming while roses fall from their lips. *Dead Girl, Driving and Other Devastations* is a triumph."—Mercedes M. Yardley, Bram Stoker Award-winning author of *Little Dead Red*

"In a debut collection weaving folklore and fairy tale and told in magical, lyrical, irresistible prose, Carina Bissett inveigles readers with the breadth of her skill. A feat of woven wonder, with spells sketched in the air and strands stretched taut, *Dead Girl, Driving and Other Devastations* is an enchanting tapestry of silken stories, the collection establishing Bissett as a world-class author of fabulism, fantasy, and horror. A must-read for lovers of Neil Gaiman, Angela Slatter, and Carmen Maria Machado." —Lee Murray, five-time Bram Stoker Award-winning author of *Grotesque: Monster Stories*

"Ravishing flights of fantasy."—Priya Sharma, Shirley Jackson Award-winning author of *All the Fabulous Beasts* and *Ormeshadow*

"Dark, often violent, *Dead Girl, Driving and Other Devastations* doesn't lie to you about the nature of its stories. Between the title page and the

Afterword lies a harrowing alliance of nightmare and fairytale. The pages are full of strange birds, resurrections, second chances, monstrous women, enchantments, and inventions. These stories explore a dark and permissive imagination, unafraid to disturb the monster at the back of the cave. It is a collection for the brave and forlorn, for those seeking escape, vengeance, transformation, or grace. There is wonder here, and freedom from shackles—for those fierce enough to wrench loose of them."—C. S. E. Cooney, World Fantasy Award-winning author of *Saint Death's Daughter*

"From fairy tale revisions to fresh takes on monstrous transitions and the absolute horrors of being female, no one knows how to write a story like Carina Bissett. Fierce yet fragile."—Lindy Ryan, author of *Bless Your Heart*

"Carina's short stories are absolutely luminous and deeply unsettling. Savour this collection like a fine blood-red wine. It's absolute perfection and will linger long after the pages are closed."—KT Wagner

CARINA BISSETT

DEAD GIRL, DRIVING

AND OTHER DEVASTATIONS

Lindy,

Enjoy the journey!

Carina Bissett

This is a work of fiction. All of the characters, names, incidents, organizations, and dialogue in this novel are either the products of the author's imagination or are used fictitiously.

The views expressed in this work are solely those of the authors and do not necessarily reflect the views of the publisher, and the publisher hereby disclaims any responsibility for them.

ISBN: 978-1-68510-123-7 (sc)
ISBN: 978-1-68510-124-4 (ebook)
Library of Congress Control Number: 2024933331

First printing edition: March 8, 2024
Printed by Trepidatio Publishing in the United States of America.
Cover Artwork: Mario Nevado – https://marionevado.art
Edited by Sean Leonard
Proofreading, Cover Layout, & Interior Layout by Scarlett R. Algee

Trepidatio Publishing, an imprint of JournalStone Publishing
3205 Sassafras Trail
Carbondale, Illinois 62901

Trepidatio books may be ordered through booksellers or by contacting:
or
JournalStone | www.journalstone.com

CONTENTS

INTRODUCTION

Somewhere inside we are all burning with rage and joy, fear and bitter disappointment. We are all living lives that force us to smooth over and box away—to contain. There is so much power, yet we let those others, those power-hungry others, hoard it for themselves. Carina Bissett's fiction claims that power in our names: the victimized and set aside, the forgotten and the unhappy, all those individuals who, unknowingly, nurture the seeds of their own transformation. Carina's stories contain elements of dark fantasy, fairytale, and folklore with more than a touch of the macabre. You will find body horror and humor alongside mythical creatures, egg babies, old gods, and clockwork women. She is what I think is best described as a fabulist.

The first time I met Carina Bissett in person was at World Fantasy Con, six years after we first started working together in an online critique group. Nothing about this meeting was a surprise. Watch Carina in a crowd. She always seems to be at the center of any group, talking, animated, and more than a little wild—just like her stories. But if you're paying attention, you'll also catch her assessing eye. She has a knife-edge understanding of humanity and a sense, always, for who any individual is at their core. In that way Carina's authorial voice exactly reflects the flesh and blood woman. She. Does. Not. Flinch.

Carina's work is distinctive both stylistically and in terms of tone, but there are definite familial ties to other authors. Her stories contain the lush language and sharply feminist perspective of Angela Carter, as well as Carter's deep understanding of fairytales and folktales. Like Shirley Jackson, Carina's fiction often explores those darkest chambers of the human psyche. Stories such as "A Seed Planted" and "Rotten" end as they should, rather than how some small part of you wishes they could. Carina's characters don't land on that single unrealistic note of happily ever after. Each story, each transformation, requires the embracing of some sort of power. And each of these transformations results in a more fully formed individual, with all the complexities that implies.

"The Certainty of Silence" is one of the standouts of this collection, but I read it for the first time almost five years ago as part of our ongoing critique group the Post Apocalyptic Writers Society (PAWS). Years later, I still remember that version of "Certainty." It was good and, better yet, distinctive, and all the right kinds of unsettling. It held so much promise. The story you'll read in these pages goes far beyond my initial hopes. "The Certainty of Silence" isn't close to standing alone. "The Gravity of Grace," also found within these pages, is one of my all-time favorite Carina Bissett stories. I loved it when I read that first unfinished draft. This final version of the story arc and character arc now rent permanent space in my head. The entire reading experience felt both surprising and inevitable--the best of all writerly hat tricks. Carina has exploded from those early seeds of "strong" and "unique" into something quite extraordinary. While it's an amazing feeling to know I helped encourage Carina along her path, in the end all Carina's accomplishments are fully her own. She is a genuine powerhouse.

Much like the characters in *Dead Girl, Driving and Other Devastations*, Carina contains layers upon layers. I've spent the last four years working with Carina on the *Dreams* anthology series. She was my assistant editor on both the *Weird Dream Society* and *Dreams for a Broken World* projects, but she was far more than the title assistant editor suggestions. Many people were involved in both projects, but Carina was my partner in crime, my sounding board, and the one who carried the belief when I started to stumble. We make a great collaborative team. As well as being a terrific editor and the best copyeditor I've ever worked with, Carina is always ready to take the next risk. Always leap, is, I've found, Carina's approach to both her fiction and her life.

Though different in content and tone, the protagonists who populate the twenty stories in *Dead Girl, Driving and Other Devastations* make their own bold choices. They jump or they slip sideways, but always there is risk involved. The journey we travel in stories like "Gaze with Undimmed Eyes and the World Drops Dead" and "Serpents and Toads" feels inevitable and compelling. A woman alone in a strange and isolated inn. A woman's deal with a devil. We read on knowing it will not go well. We read on waiting for the four-lane pileup. And in Carina's deft hands, we are never disappointed. The endings of these stories are gloriously unsettling crashes.

Whether it's science fiction, gothic fairytale, dark fantasy, or absurdist, the world—Carina's many worlds—aren't about hope, or forgiveness, or even acceptance. They're about power struggles and familial and societal oppression, and, in many of her stories, the ways in which women must become seeming monsters to express their true authentic selves. Her fiction is, like Carina, unapologetic, bold, and most importantly complicated—in the very best of ways.

Some of Carina's stories eviscerate the too-often dysfunctional family. Whether it concerns the impact of having a fairy godmother who is also a goddess of death in "Dead Girl, Driving" or the experiences of a girl with a mythological bird for a mother and an ancient, bloodthirsty god figure for a father in "The Gravity of Grace," the center of the story is deeper than the individual character's journey of transformation. The flawed familial dynamics are the center from which everything else emerges. No one in these stories is entirely pure and those who inhabit evil, we come to understand, have a perspective, however skewed, that makes sense.

It's not just family: stories like "The Stages of Monster Grief: A Guide for Middle-Aged Vampires" and "Cracked" focus on how society's expectations inevitably create middle-aged female vampires and women whose children are oversized decorated eggs. And best of all, it always makes sense.

Whether humorous or viscerally unsettling, like Carina, each story in this collection is powered by slow burning, transformative rage.

Many of the protagonists in this collection are literal monsters, or at least see themselves as such. And then there are the psychological monsters who lack emotional connection—those self-absorbed creators of chaos who fling open Pandora's box. And yet these people love. They somehow dance just along the edges of compassion. Or to put it another way: Carina takes our everyday monstrous choices—to ignore the impact our actions or lack of actions have—and manifests the emotional truth of these moments through the lens of her characters. And how can it be otherwise when there is almost always a cost that must be paid for even small threads of connection and caring? These people are always pushed to remain separate from their supposed tribe.

Like her characters, like all of us, Carina's creative vision is driven by forces she's honed over the course of years. She has lived a life that has gifted her nothing. Instead, she's been forced, despite her brilliant creativity, to chisel out each stone step on her personal and artistic journey. Of course, Carina as an author doesn't flinch or soften. She is truth and power. She drags you, the reader, into a seeming nightmare and then forces you to take note of the beauty found there.

I read the entire collection quickly. I couldn't help myself. Once I started it was incredibly difficult to set these experiences aside. It isn't so much the depth of her knowledge regarding fairytales and folklore, or even the knowledge she's gained from teaching other writers how to successfully harness those ancient stories. The strength of *Dead Girl, Driving and Other Devastations* lies in the feral imagination Carina applies to her understanding of the human condition and the psychic wounds we all bear. She creates fire on the page. Stories as conflagrations. Stories as insurrectionary reimaginings and burning condemnations. Stories you'll carry with you long after you finish the last page.

—Julie C. Day

DEAD GIRL, DRIVING

AND OTHER DEVASTATIONS

DEAD GIRL, DRIVING

My boyfriend killed me.

Of course, he did. My seventh death. Too bad for him it backfired. That was the real shocker. The bruises around my throat faded and bloomed like a collar of black roses on Brody, instead. My godmother had changed the rules, and I didn't know what that meant.

I gagged a little as I came back to life.

"Goddammit!" I shook my fist at the ceiling of our ratty apartment, even though the one I cursed didn't live in no heaven. A crack ripped across the old plaster. "This ain't none of your business."

Beaks rapped at the third-story window. Seven crows there to witness Brody flailing against invisible forces strangling him as he'd done to me. One last kick and Brody went limp. The birds' incessant tapping abruptly stopped.

The back of my throat tickled. I coughed up a black feather, followed by six more.

"This is going too far." I yelled. "It's not supposed to work like this, and you know it!"

The room stayed as silent as a tomb.

I chucked a half-empty bottle of whiskey at the window and missed. Damned glass didn't even break. The crows fanned their feathers and danced on the sill. Cheeky birds.

I lit a cigarette and crouched down next to Brody on the orange shag carpet. "You stupid shit."

The crows bobbed back and forth from their perch. I ignored them. *Seven for a secret never to be told.* Brody's blue eyes stayed fixed on the cracked ceiling. Some secret. I took another drag and then stubbed the cig out on the shag. I reckoned it was past time for a road trip. Godmother Death and I had unfinished business.

***

The first time I died, my godmother saved me. Easy as snapping her fingers. Not that I asked to be saved, any more than I asked to be born.

She told me the truth of it on my seventh birthday. I'd stolen one of those packaged cupcakes from the corner store, and I already had a candle, the same I used for all my birthdays—a big number one. It still held traces of pink wax, but the color darkened with each use. The other 364 days of the year, I kept it wrapped in a bit of newspaper with my mother's name and a few short lines about her equally short life. I kept it, along with a few other treasured possessions, in a tattered cigar box that might have once belonged to my father. Bastard made it a whole year as single parent before taking off for a fresh new life. Left me behind. In my dreams, a black-winged angel told me not to worry about that piece of trash. I was better off without him. Maybe she was right, but what kid wants to hear that?

I'd been in foster care ever since. Never stayed long in one place, so there wasn't much to remember until my seventh birthday—the day *she* showed up. I'd been placed with the Raffertys, who had more foster kids than common sense, and I'd escaped the noise of the house in the alleyway out back. It was cold and it was dark in the place where I'd taken refuge, but I struck a pilfered Zippo to life and fired up that birthday candle. Wishes tumbled round and round in the back of my throat.

In the end, I settled on a fairy godmother. Nothing like wishing for more wishes, right? I held on to that real tight and blew out the flame flickering in and out of existence. And then, she was suddenly there—Godmother Death dressed in a concert T-shirt, tight jeans, and Doc Martens—the black-winged angel who kept me safe in my dreams. No wishes for me. Oh, no. My godmother sat me down with the truth, instead. When she'd shown up on the hour of my birth, I'd killed my mother and been born dead to boot. Something about me plucked at Death's heartstrings though, and she did the unthinkable. I started breathing again. Just like that.

A crow dropped down from the moon and landed on my godmother's shoulder. Godmother Death frowned and unfolded wings of her own. She ruffled her feathers, and the crow took flight once more.

"Listen to me, girl." Her eyes were black as jet. "Stop thinking about that no-good father of yours or how bad you think you've got it. There are millions worse off than you."

The night warped, folding in on itself as a door to a different dimension opened. One long, lonely road bisected a desolate landscape behind her. Godmother Death rose from the ground. Dust and debris swirled in the alleyway. The candle fell off the cupcake and landed on cracked asphalt.

"I gave you a second chance. Concentrate on making a future of your own," she said. "Don't fuck it up."

Just what every seven-year-old wants to hear on their birthday.

The night swallowed her, and she went back to whatever place she'd come from. A single black feather stuck up straight from the smashed ruins of chocolate cake.

Ain't life a bitch.

***

Dragging a body down three flights of stairs was no joke. By the time I reached the landing on the second floor, I decided a banged-up body was the least of Brody's problems, so I kicked him down, one step at a time. When we reached the bottom, he looked as battered as I felt. I rolled him over.

"Jesus, Mary, and Joseph," I said when I saw what was left of his face. A leftover curse picked up from one of my fosters. Maybe the Raffertys. Can't remember.

The crows swooped down to check out his flayed cheeks.

"You leave him be!"

They circled up a storm, cawin' and clackin' about him not being left out as a snack.

But I hadn't given up yet. It wasn't his fault he loved me too much. He'd never wanted to hurt me. Said it'd never happen again. Said it more than once. And then he lost control. Stupid prick didn't listen about Godmother Death. I bet he wished he'd paid more attention. Can't say I didn't warn him.

I shook my fist at the circling birds and ran to the carport. Didn't bother much with the fancy car cover. Left it where it lay and backed up to collect Brody. The trunk was full of speakers, tools, and an unused gym bag, so I shoved him in the passenger seat. The crows landed on the flaming Firebird spread across that shiny, black hood. Dude loved that car. He'd have killed me all over again if he knew I'd dared to sit behind the wheel.

I adjusted the rear-view mirror and grinned a little. I revved the engine. The crows took off in one big tornado of feathers. They left runnels of shit streaked across the windshield, but I countered with a spray of blue mist and a few swipes of the windshield wipers. Godmother

Death could express her displeasure all she wanted, but we needed to have another sit-down.

This time, on my terms.

***

It was the boy near the corner mart who killed me the second time—just a few months after my thirteenth birthday. He looked like a crow in human form, all swoopy black bangs and a hankering for shiny things. The crow boy spent every day folding paper animals, a whole origami zoo filled with fun. Ice, smack, blow. Dude was diverse. Sometimes, when business was slow, he'd dig out one of those packets and carefully unfold it to dust his nose.

Three stories up, the fire escape of the old brick apartment belonged to me. As the oldest foster kid there, I claimed that square of steel grating as my own. But I didn't end up staying with that family for long. I couldn't resist the promise of a good time, so I made a trade behind the dumpster. Started out fun, but it went sideways—fast. I came back. He didn't.

Godmother Death was waiting when I returned to the living, and she was pissed as I'd ever seen her, wings spread wide enough to block the full moon. A black bird balanced on each shoulder. Blood trickled from her nose, and she was none too happy about that.

"Stupid girl." She wiped the smear from her upper lip with the back of her hand. "What have you gotten yourself into?"

I pulled my knees to my chest. My heart hammered like I'd been sprinting.

"What are you doing hanging around *this*?" Godmother Death kicked the crow boy's foot. "You should know better."

My stomach lurched.

"What happened?" My voice slurred like I'd slammed a six-pack of wine coolers, and maybe I had.

"What *happened*? What do you *think* happened?" Godmother Death beat her wings twice in agitation. Her feet hovered above the ground for a moment. The blast of wind sent paper tigers tumbling down the alley. "You died. *Again*."

I fought back another wave of nausea. "What about him?"

"Same as you. Just a few minutes earlier. Respiratory failure."

I licked my lips. A trace of bitterness crawled across my tongue. "You can bring him back too, right?"

Godmother Death laughed, a sharp slicing sound that almost made me wish I was dead again. "Don't be ridiculous. That one did it to himself." She made another pass at the blood still trickling from her nose, wiped her hand on her jeans. "But you, well you're my responsibility."

My godmother spent a good hour lecturing me behind that overflowing dumpster in the back alley. Put me in my place. Bad decisions. *That* talk. Whatever. The whole time, I couldn't stop looking at the dead boy slumped against the dirty brick. In the end, I didn't blame him, not really. Accidents happen.

***

I disguised Brody as best I could with a baseball hat and a jacket draped across his chest. The drive-through cashier at the burger joint just nodded as I rattled off the deets while collecting a bag of fries and a soda. Drunk boyfriend picked a fight. Got his ass kicked. Sleeping it off. Mostly true, anyhow. The trip was quiet, other than that. Even so, I paused at the turn off to the Devil's Highway. I was ninety-nine percent certain I'd guessed right. Fit with Godmother Death's sense of humor. Damned if she didn't make me cross it, back and forth, three times before the right road finally opened under the Firebird's custom rims. But when she did, the long, grey stretch of old asphalt reached out as far as I could see.

Every now and then, I checked on Brody. He mostly smelled like blood and sweat and piss. But if I breathed deep enough, I could catch a hint of those sweet cigarillos he loved so much. He stared out the window and said nothing. Best date ever.

***

My third death was deliberate. Cut my wrists on my fifteenth birthday. One of those things, you know? I'd been thinking about it for a while. I mean, really, how many times would *she* bring me back? I was dog-tired. Sick of life. Sick of guilt. Sick of shadows.

No one tells you how much it hurts, or how long it takes. I even did my research, used the straight razor to cut the veins the long ways.

But first, I popped pills. A whole bottle of them washed down with a few swigs of cheap vodka as I filled up the bathtub with hot water. It was my birthday, after all. I even dropped in a fizzy bath bomb that smelled like those big, white flowers people leave on graves. When the bath salts petered out and the room was good and steamy, I made a quick slash on my left wrist. Hurt like a motherfucker, but I did the right one, too, even though the second cut veered off course. A little more haphazard than I'd imagined, but then again nothing ever turned out right for me. I closed my eyes and counted down. *One for sorrow. Two for joy.*

The water was still warm when Godmother Death showed up.

My heart stuttered back to life and started to beat strong and steady.

"You've gone and done it now, girl." She stepped out of the mirror into the mist. Her wings filled the room. Fresh blood stained her upper lip. She was still dressed in jeans and a T-shirt, but this time her arms were covered with a black leather jacket. "Not very efficient."

"I wasn't sure you'd come." My tongue felt heavy.

Godmother Death scowled and kicked the empty pill bottle. "*This* wasn't enough to do more than damage your kidneys. Thanks for that," she said wryly.

The blood reversed its course. The veins sealed shut without even the trace of a scar left as a reminder.

I wanted to ask if she loved me, but the words got stuck in my throat. I scowled, instead. "Took you long enough."

Two crows fluttered up from the puke green vanity to the rusted shower rod. A third hopped from the chipped toilet tank to the tub spout. The bird clucked disapprovingly and leaned forward as if preparing to drop a load in my bath.

"Don't you dare!"

The feathered fiend chortled, and its buddies joined in, setting up a ruckus sure to wake the entire house. And how I was supposed to explain that?

Godmother Death sighed and folded her wings nice and neat behind her back. "What am I going to do with you?"

"Take me with you?" The water cleared, but that flowery perfume from the bath salts still hung thick in the air.

"It doesn't work like that." My godmother tucked her hands in her pockets, but not before I saw the slick red around her wrists. "Pull yourself together, girl. You can get through this. Trust me. You have more to live for than you think."

"You know something I don't?" I couldn't conceal the bitterness. "Look around. My life isn't worth a shit."

The crows took flight, black feathers filling the cramped room.

"Take me with you." That time I wasn't asking.

"This path you're on leads to no good. You're better than this. Trust me."

Was that the shimmer of tears?

"Please," Godmother Death said. "Try a little harder. For me."

When the steam cleared, I was alone. The liquor bottle, pill container, and razor blade were gone, too. Three black feathers drifted down to float in the water around my knobby knees. I plucked them out one by one and laid them out to dry.

***

The Firebird ran out of gas sometime after the right road opened, but it didn't matter. The wheels kept spinning. Miles ticked by. The car steered itself.

A waiting game.

I had nowhere else to be, so I selected a loop of heavy metal, turned up the volume, and settled back until Godmother Death saw fit to finish the stand-off.

Crows perched on fence posts, buzzed past the car, circled overhead. Not the whole lot of them, just a few at a time. When I finally saw all seven, flying in a V like a winged arrow overhead, I smiled. Brody smiled, too. It's amazing what you can do with a crumpled up fast-food bag and a Sharpie.

A house came into view at the end of the road. Not a mansion or a castle like I'd envisioned so many times in the past, but a cozy cottage all snuggled up to the base of towering cliffs that stretched off into the distance on either side. The car slowed until it was barely creeping forward. I could've walked faster. The crows fanned their tail feathers and skimmed ahead, landing on the hood as the car finally rolled to a stop.

The cottage door stood wide open, but there was no one waiting. The crows took flight once more, swooping into the cottage, one by one. The radio signal scrambled, so I flipped off the stereo and shouldered the weight of the heavy silence. I lit a cig and stared at that open door for a while, wondering what I'd find inside.

"Well, shit." I stubbed out the cherry on the dashboard. "Not lookin' good dude." I flicked the butt out the window. "Don't go anywhere. I'll be right back."

***

After that failed attempt in the bathroom, I killed myself three more times before I finally gave up. Godmother Death's visits in my dreams came further and further apart, and I never again saw her in the real world even though others around me claimed they had.

I don't remember much about my second attempt. I'd been trying to outrun nightmares, and between one moment and the next, I turned the steering wheel of my old junker real hard, crossing the blur of yellow lines and driving straight into the oversized headlights of a semi headed the opposite direction.

Ribs crushed, collarbone buckled, but that old car was solid as a tank. Don't remember much more than the sound of metal hitting metal and the explosion. I thought that was some dumb stunt that only happened in the movies. If I'd known, I sure as hell wouldn't have picked that door. Burning is not an easy way to go. Trust me on that shit.

Rubberneckers stopped, watched the whole thing. Guess the fire was too hot for anyone to help me, but the trucker escaped. I saw him later, sitting in the back of an ambulance, wrapped in a tinfoil blanket and sucking down oxygen. His eyes were hollow as fishing holes cut in a frozen lake. Dude looked like he might never recover. I decided, then and there, never to do that again.

Eyewitnesses said an angel carried me out of the flames. There hadn't been anything left of me that wasn't broken or burned. But by the time that angel laid me down on the side of the road, I looked good as new. Some said the angel flew back up to heaven. Others said she turned into ash. But they all agreed there were crows screaming and circling the scene. A whole murder of them.

The next time, I made sure no one was around. Swam out as far as I could into the biggest lake I could find. I ain't no swimmer to begin with so it didn't take long 'til I couldn't swim any farther. Panic hit when my lungs filled up with water. I thrashed around, going nowhere fast, until I blacked out. Godmother Death left me on the shore of that lake. I woke covered in a black leather jacket that smelled like smoke. Underneath, I found five shiny black feathers fanned out on my chest.

I made it a whole two years after that. Did pretty good, too. Then that old, familiar feeling crept back in, and I found myself at the top of a fifteen-story building with a stolen key card in my hand. Before I could change my mind, I climbed over the railing, and took that leap of faith, man. Flew so high, I almost touched the sky. And then gravity kicked in, tugging all that soft, pink meat down to the street below. I came back to life feeling more beat up than the other times I'd kicked it, but I climbed off the roof of that crushed car as fast as I could. Didn't want anyone to stop me. After the semi-truck incident, I'd blathered on about Godmother Death to the wrong people, and I never wanted to repeat that mistake. Spent time in a hospital with its sad-sack counsellors and white-collared penguins all calling for salvation. But no one there could help me. Not really.

A few blocks down the street, my limp went away. The soft spot on the back of my head rounded out, and my right shoulder popped and twisted back in place. Took all I had not to scream. The bruises started to fade to a sickly greenish black. I figured they were barely visible under the dingy streetlights, but to be safe, I ducked into a corner bar that promised to be even darker inside.

I slid onto a cracked vinyl barstool next to a guy who appeared to be watching everyone at once. He was all angles and sharp edges. In a way, he reminded me of my crow boy, and I was in a wicked need for a line of smack and a shot or two. I always came back from being dead cold sober, something I needed to remedy as soon as possible.

The man took a good long look at me—torn clothes, bruises, and all. "Girl, you look as though you've been to hell and back."

Without asking for permission, I picked up the full shot glass next to his beer and slammed it. The welcome warmth of whiskey burned all the way down.

The man took a drag off a slender cigarillo. The sticky-sweet smell made my mouth water. His blue eyes sparkled, as he waved for the bartender to serve up another round.

He exhaled, smoke all tangled in syllables. "My name's Brody."

We clinked glasses, and that was that.

***

I walked into Godmother Death's cottage like I owned the damned place. But except for the clackin' and cawin', it was as quiet as anywhere I'd ever been. I followed the crows to an arch cut straight into the cliffs forming the back wall. The closer I got, the brighter the light. I might've been a little anxious, but I stepped over that threshold even though everything screamed at me to run—run far, far away.

Don't know what I expected, not really, but it sure wasn't what I found. Small niches had been carved into the stone, and every one of them had a candle nestled inside. Not all were burning, but enough of them were lit to reveal the figure of Godmother Death lying on the floor, all crumpled up. Even her wings were broken, bent in the wrong places.

My knees wobbled, but I rushed to her anyway. I ran forever, each step stretching like that long, grey road. Seven crows circled overhead like a storm pushed to breaking.

"Godmother!"

I knelt down beside her and reached out, but there wasn't a single part of her I could touch, not an inch that wasn't broken, bruised, or burned. Blood still dripped from what remained of her nose. Wet red streamed like ribbons from the cuts on her wrists. The pieces of her not charbroiled were crushed or bloated. There was a reason she hadn't let me see her for so long. She'd been hiding all those wounds, every damned one caused by me.

Godmother Death opened her eyes. She coughed long and loud, a muddy gush of lake water spilled from bruised lips.

"You shouldn't have come."

But I had, and I'd hauled Brody along with me. Had she traded his life for mine? It didn't look like she'd survive much longer, let alone bring Brody back. But I couldn't leave her like that. There was no turning around. No other options.

I pulled my T-shirt off and tried to wipe the mess off Godmother Death's face, but she was *all* mess and I only had one shirt. She grabbed my wrist.

"Listen to me, girl. I know why you're here." Her eyes were bloodshot, thin red lines radiating from irises dark as death.

"I came to visit my godmother," I said, pushing the words past the knot in my throat. "I've missed you."

"You reminded me of someone that night at the hospital. I remembered a time…" Godmother Death coughed; her sides heaved as she tried to catch her breath. "I couldn't save…you…I thought I could. Do some good. But I've got nothing left."

"So you took Brody instead."

Godmother Death grinned. Her teeth were covered in fresh blood. "Don't feel sorry for him. *That* man paid his dues."

She pushed one wing aside, revealing a burnt-out candle. A wisp of smoke spiralled up. It smelled sweet as a cigarillo. I fiddled with the Zippo, my good luck charm. One flick and I could light that candle again. She couldn't stop me. But then I thought of Brody's hands around my neck and realized I didn't want to.

The crows got louder, dropped closer. The wall of flames flickered from the wind thrown off their wings.

"There are rules that come with great responsibility. I accepted that, and then I broke them. Willingly." Godmother Death coughed, wiped her knuckles across her lips. "You always have a choice. Remember that."

"I'm sorry." My cheeks were wet. And even though I'd never cried, not once, I knew what that meant. "I'll do better. Give me one more chance."

A half circle of candles flared to life in an empty alcove behind her.

"You have seven." Her arm fell to the floor of the cave with a thud.

A crow dropped from the cyclone of glossy black wings and dove straight down, right towards Godmother Death. A door opened in her chest, and the bird disappeared. I stood and backed away, as each of the six remaining crows followed the first.

The flames on the burning candles rose high and then higher still. Godmother Death folded in on herself until she wasn't much more than a bundle of black feathers and delicate bones. The newly formed bird cocked its head and looked at me with those endlessly black eyes. *One for sorrow.* The crow hopped towards me and opened its wings. I dropped my hands to my sides, palms facing up.

"I love you, too, Godmother."

That's all it took. The crow leapt up and soared straight for me. A door opened in my chest, and the crow passed through. Can't say it didn't hurt a little 'cause love sometimes comes with pain, but it wasn't more than I could handle. Wings pushed their way from between my shoulders and I flexed them, fanning the flames of the souls still living in the outside world. It would be so easy to blow them all out. Harder to keep them burning, I suppose. In any case, I would figure it out with my godmother safe in my heart.

Now it was my turn.

THE STAGES OF MONSTER GRIEF: A GUIDE FOR MIDDLE-AGED VAMPIRES

Ladies, you may have dreamed of a day when you no longer have to "age gracefully" or are forced into obscurity by a wardrobe filled with basic neutrals. You look in the mirror only to be confronted with sagging skin, pebbled cellulite, and wrinkles in places you never expected. You start to wonder if you'll be old and alone forever. A little bit of blood is worth the price to drink at the fountain of youth, isn't it?

1. Denial

And then it happens: some figure seduces you from the shadows, and you fall lovingly into their arms with your throat bared by a torn turtleneck. You think you've beaten the odds. Only, death is never as romantic as it is in the movies, and rebirth is downright disgusting. That two hundred dollar cut and color is reduced to a dirt-matted mop, and your nails are broken from digging your way out of a shallow grave. Don't even get started on the state of your skin. And *they* say mud makes a magical facial. Call bullshit on that one.

You blow it off, decide you were slipped a mickey, and some teenage asshat buried your passed out body in a mound of moldy leaves as a joke. No Prince Charming dressed like Bela Lugosi. No sexy interlude behind the cocktail lounge. No throb of the forbidden. You refuse to acknowledge the truth. So, you rub at the bruise on your neck and search through the closet for an even higher collar to hide the arterial bloom.

The next day, you call in sick. After all, you've been working at the college, wearing your nicest smile for twenty fucking years. Don't you deserve some time off for good behavior? You've never acted on the impulse to fail a student just because they are a monster in the classroom. But no one has ever thanked you—not once. Screw that.

When you wake up, the day has disappeared and September's Harvest Moon squats low on the horizon. You've been eating vegan in an attempt to lose belly fat and to reduce cholesterol, but all you can think about is a nice, juicy steak. Rare. And why shouldn't you treat yourself? You only live once, right?

2. Anger

Okay, so maybe you didn't make it to the restaurant on your walk from campus to downtown. And those belligerent frat boys probably had it coming, anyway.

Back at home, you take a shower and toss your blood-soaked clothes in the bin. No more beige for you. From here on out, you will only wear velvet and lace, cut seductively to show off the new you. But, when you look in the mirror, nothing has changed. That crepey skin is still visible on your neck, your breasts sag without the support of an underwire, and the cellulite on your thighs appears even more dimpled than it did before.

You go out the next night looking for answers from your vampire progenitor. You figure they have some explaining to do. Why can you see yourself in a mirror? Better yet, where's the god-damn fountain of youth? You wouldn't have wanted the cursed blessing if you knew that you'd have to spend the rest of your presumably immortal days alone at the resting age of fifty-five. What kind of sick fuck would damn you to that particular purgatory?

3. Depression

You think about walking outside and ending it all with a little vitamin D, but you've never liked the sun—skin cancer and all of that. You didn't wear wide-brimmed hats, long sleeves, and your weight in SPF 100 for thirty years to go out in a blaze of glory.

Instead, you go on a binge of boys and booze.

It could be worse.

4. Acceptance

You invest in corsets, light your home with candles. Still, it takes some time to let go of modern perceptions of youth and beauty, even though you know from experience there's more to life than that.

After all, you can deadlift a family sedan. You've gotten out of the academic grind with a few well-placed casualties. And snapshots of your new, "I don't give a fuck" stylings turned you into an Instagram hit. Sure, those pictures are mistakenly titled "Sexy at Sixty," but whatever.

It doesn't take long before your memoir is sold as fiction for six-figures, and you start the popular blog "So You Want to Write a Vampire Novel." In between readings and convention appearances, you stalk the streets looking for one of your own kind. Even though you never found the vampire who turned you (or any other vampire for that matter), you crave a companion. So, when you see the foxy woman astride a black beast of a motorcycle, silver hair streaming out behind her, you act on impulse.

You pretend you didn't notice it was a full moon, or that the howls dogging her trail sounded like wolves.

It's your nature after all, you tell yourself as you dig a shallow grave with a broken fender. You tell yourself that she'll love you forever even as you push the dirt over her drained body. She'll forget her lover with the moon-bright eyes. She'll forget the spat that sent her far from her pack. Your blood will triumph; you're sure of it. But when she rises, the silver-haired woman looks right through you.

She stumbles away and leaves you behind to stare at an empty hole filled with nothing more than moonlight and frost.

Over the distant sounds of traffic and sirens, a wolf howls.

5. Betrayal

Overhead, January's Wolf Moon watches with an amused grin. The silver-haired woman breaks into a lope.

You don't need a magic mirror to tell you how this will play out. The movies are full of stories about romantic triangles and unrequited love. If nothing else, you'll no longer be alone. You gather your cape. And follow.

TWICE IN THE TELLING

They say I killed my sister, that I pulled her over the railing into the swollen river. They say my sister struggled up until the very end. They say I crushed her bones with my strong brown arms, scalped the shining hair from her skull. Some claim I'm an ogress, a kelpie, a nokken, that I'm no sister at all.

Maybe they are right.

Or maybe, just maybe, the ballad is only the beginning.

***

Our mother found me at the water's edge, dressed in nothing more than river weed. She left her basket of berries behind, strapped me alongside her first-born daughter, and returned to the husband waiting at home near the mill pond.

Years later she died, our mother, as so many mothers do. A late birthing turned wrong. We were only children ourselves at the time, but we remembered her face, my sister Twyla and I. Together, we kept her memory alive. I traced her features on the mill pond's surface each morning and again each night as I swam round and round, savoring the familiar feel of water against my thick skin. Twyla waited on the muddy bank where she wove reeds and grass into the shape of our mother's body. If you knew where to look, you could find our mother everywhere—watching over us.

But sometimes watching isn't enough.

***

Our father couldn't bear the sight of his daughters, Twyla fair as her bonny mother, and the changeling child, the shadow that had stolen his dead wife's heart. Yet he kept his promise to honor a mother's dying wish to protect *both* her daughters. Instead of sending me away, he turned his attention back to his work and left us to do as we pleased. The townies knew the miller's daughters had free rein, but they whispered, even then, of my mud-stained hems always dripping, of the way I kept my golden sister within constant hands-grasp. Even before we shifted from girls to women, the boys stayed out of reach of my iron-sharp nails and venomous teeth. They learned early on that the safest place to admire my beautiful sister was from a distance.

A few even had the scars to prove it.

***

And then, one summer day, a traveling prince heard rumors of the miller's daughter and her hair of gold. He shifted course to quell his curiosity, but my sister and I spied him on the road and fled to the safety of the first of three bridges leading from our humble town to the wide world beyond. My shadow loomed large, filling the space as I attempted to shield my treasured Twyla. Horse hooves clomped heavily overhead.

One stopped at the top of the stone arch. The pond's overflow trickled at our feet, a welcome cover muffling my sister's gasping breaths. I held her close and waited until the horses and their riders returned the way they had come. We spent the night there in the mud, my arms wrapped around Twyla's shaking form. I kissed her shining brow and vowed to keep her safe.

For a while, I even believed I could.

***

The second time, the prince nearly caught us.

We were laying, head-to-head, on the pond's far bank and did not hear the horses approach until they were nearly upon us. The reeds provided cover, but the prince would find us soon enough.

I slid into the pond and beckoned Twyla to follow. She rolled on her stomach and shook her head ever so slightly. Hanging from her ears, tiny silver bells tinkled. I scooped up a handful of mud and reached forward to slick the cover of darkness over her lustrous hair. Tears ran down her cheeks. I grasped her hands in mine, resisting the temptation to pull her into my watery domain despite her fears.

A man's deep baritone sent a pair of trumpeter swans to wing. "There's nothing here, your Highness."

More than anything, I wished Twyla and I could follow the birds to the safety of the sky, but I was a creature of water, not air. My sister a creature bound to land.

"Look harder," the prince commanded. Tack jangled. Leather creaked.

Our father had finally betrayed our mother's final wish. How else could the prince have known where to find us?

I traced the shape of the three bridges on my sister's forearm, and then pressed two fingers to my lips. Two sisters. Two bridges.

Twyla nodded. I smiled encouragingly and sank beneath the still water. When I reemerged near the fields, I held a burnished carp in each hand. Their scales glittered in the mid-day sun, and I splashed them against the water's surface to draw the men's attention.

I led the prince and his men on a wild chase through bracken and bramble before turning back towards the mill, a place where a frightened daughter might try to hide. I left the carp on the front steps of our father's cottage. A handprint of golden scales smeared the hide of the old black mare I sent galloping across the field. I grinned at the sight.

Twyla waited for me at the second bridge, where the run-off from the mill pond joined the brook. We spent the night in a tree, tied to one another with our long, trailing locks—gold and black bound as tightly as our souls, sisters in every way that mattered.

In the morning, I washed the muck from Twyla's hair and sang our mother's favorite songs. My glorious sister was a person, not a thing to be owned. Why could our father not see that?

I would keep Twyla safe. There was no one else left.

***

We made our way downstream, to the place where our familiar brook fed into a river. Our mother cautioned us to never go past the second bridge, but we decided she would have changed her mind if she'd known the circumstances. She might have even joined us. The way was long and treacherous. We followed the flow as it grew larger and larger. Finally, we reached a point where we could barely see the opposite bank. The river took the easy way as it wound through rolling hills overflowing with bracken and brambles. A few hours later, we reached the third bridge and the road that led to the outside world.

"This is where Mother found you." Twyla's fingers entwined with my own.

I flinched. This topic was taboo. "You don't know that."

Twyla looked at me with eyes the color of an afternoon storm. "Why else would she forbid it?"

She was speaking of the summer before our mother died, when we snuck out of the cottage to follow her.

The best berries grew near the third bridge. Our mother was the only one who knew the location of a particular patch where the fruit carried the taste of old magic. She sold her pots of jam for silver. People came far and wide for the pleasure of tasting the annual bounty of that blue-black fruit, though I'd been forbidden to taste a single drop.

When she discovered us lurking in the tall grasses near the third bridge, she'd left her baskets behind once more and led us back home. Our mother sobbed the entire night. Listening, Twyla and I vowed we would never disobey her again.

Yet there we were. Twyla plucked a few berries from their hiding place deep inside a bush so twisted and dark, I'd assumed it was dead. Each globe was no bigger than a thumbnail. Curved hooks protected the bounty, but Twyla crushed the berries anyway. The fruit's black juice mingled with her bright red blood. The sight made me dizzy, and I trembled at the sound of water crashing over rocks. I shook my head and reached out to steady myself. The bush bit back.

I withdrew my hand. Instead of the blue-black that marked my sister's palm, the juice gleamed green as river moss against the burnished color of my skin.

"What is this?" I swiped my hand against my skirt, but the stain remained.

"Proof," said my sister. "This is where you belong."

A bugle sounded. Dogs barked. They'd found us.

I grabbed Twyla by the hand and dragged her up the embankment to the road. If we crossed the bridge, perhaps, we could lose them further downstream. I tried and failed to remember fragments of overheard conversations, something about crossing water and covering tracks.

Together, we ran barefoot along the stone road that crossed the river.

This bridge was five times the length of the other two bridges combined. It felt as though we could run forever and never make it across. When we reached the apex, we realized the truth was even more awful. Mounted soldiers blocked the way to shore. We turned to flee back from where we'd come, but that retreat was barred as well. The prince had found his prize.

Still sticky with fruit and blood, our hands linked, and I pulled Twyla to the railing. She hesitated but followed. The river below thrashed with fierce intensity, a far cry from the familiar mill pond. But water was water, or so I told myself, and I was an excellent swimmer.

"It's the only way," I said.

Twyla's face was as pale as sun-bleached sheets. From their place on her delicate earlobes, the silver bells shivered. "I can't, sister."

"You must."

This time she trusted me, and we leapt from the bridge, hand-in hand. The prince's shout was a mere whisper above the crashing sound of the waves.

***

The river roared. It pulled us down, down to the darkest depths. It pummeled. It bruised. It called out in a voice both familiar and foreign.

My back scraped sharp rocks lurking at the bottom. They tore at my clothes, ripped them off piece by piece. The water tickled the soles of my feet, caressed my thighs, licked the inside of my wrists. It pried at my eyes, stung my ears with demands that I *listen*, return to the realm where I belonged.

When I couldn't stand it a moment longer, I opened my mouth. The water rushed in, filled me up. And with it came a flood of ancestral memories that scoured away all pretense of humanity.

I covered my ears—both hands my own.

I had lost her, Twyla, my beautiful, brave sister.

***

I finally found her, far downstream. A man was crouched at her side. Still submerged, I watched him from behind a large boulder crowned in a glorious coat of moss. The man was dressed for long travel. He had a harp slung across his back. A leather bag leaned next to the trunk of a towering cottonwood. He hummed a tune I did not recognize, the melancholy notes occasionally accompanied with words. His voice caught on a sob, and he reached out a trembling hand to touch the halo of golden hair splayed around Twyla's head.

That a stranger would dare to touch my sister sent a cold rage pummeling through my veins. I emerged as naked as the day our mother had found me. River weed clung to my hair, slicked against my skin, and hung in a tangle past my waist.

A pile of pebbles shifted under the weight of webbed feet. The rattling sound intruded just enough to give the harper pause. He slowly looked over his shoulder as though expecting to find a raccoon or another familiar predator. His eyes widened when that predator proved to be me.

"Holy mother of God."

I bared my teeth and splayed fingers tipped with razor-sharp nails. The stranger fled, leaving behind his leather bag in his haste. I considered following him, dragging him back to the river and drowning him in the dark depths. But Twyla had been left alone far too long as it was, so I ignored temptation and went to kneel at her side.

Death was not an unfamiliar sight. My sister and I had once stood like sentinels on either side of our mother's bed as she passed from this world. There'd been others, too. Rabbits snared in the reeds. Birds crushed while still forming inside their shells. Rats drowned in the still mill pond. But nothing prepared me for the sight of my beautiful sister flayed open as though she was a trophy the river had gleefully unwrapped.

She had struggled up until the very end, her nails broken and caked with silt. Her dress was in tatters, and her skin had been peeled back to expose tendon and bone. The only thing that remained untarnished was her shining hair and the silver bells adorning her perfectly shaped ears, which were so unlike my own.

I pulled Twyla into my lap, crushed her to my chest with my strong brown arms. Her head lolled brokenly, and her one remaining eye looked past me to the bright blue bowl of sky. All I could think about was the harper's song. A plan slowly took shape.

That night, I guarded my sister's body. Not even a bear would dare to try and take her from me. The next morning, I went to work. I crushed her bones, separating the knuckles for tuning pegs, the breastbone fitted as a soundboard. I scalped the shining hair from her head, carefully washed it, and stretched the strands taut on the bone harp to dry. The bells now pieced my own ears. She would walk with me, every step a reminder of all that had been lost. I committed the remains to the river, secure in an underwater barrow until I could return.

In the meantime, there was a murderer to catch.

***

It took three days before I was able to set out, not that anyone could have recognized me as the girl I once was.

I had shorn my hair and left it in Twyla's barrow to keep her company in my absence. The harper's bag contained a change of clothes, and I found that the guise of a man suited me just fine. A cloak covered that which I could not otherwise mask.

It didn't take long to locate the prince's path. Forced adulation marked his passing, but then the wandering harper's tracks merged with his, and triumph turned to tragedy in the bard's shared song.

Oh yonder stands the prince, my love,
Binnorie, O Binnorie;
My sister plots to take my place;

By the bonny mill-dams o' Binnorie.
She drowned me, threw me off the bridge;
Binnorie, O Binnorie.

"The poor prince," said the people. "To lose his love so."

The bone harp shivered but stayed silent. Twyla's silver bells whispered words for me alone to hear, but it wasn't enough to block the lies spreading like a stain before us.

"What a wicked sister," the townspeople muttered. "A monster."

An ogress lurking in the mud under a great stone bridge. A kelpie in the guise of a horse, black as night. A nokken with webbed toes and a hunger for human hearts. The story shifted depending on the teller, but some things stayed the same:

There were once two sisters. And now there was but one.

***

The prince continued along the river road to the kingdom near the sea. The crowds grew in each passing town. White silk streamers and late summer flowers greeted the traveling retinue and the prince destined to join two countries in wedded bliss. In return, he left a stain behind in each hamlet and home he deigned to visit. Sometimes, he left several.

I delayed my pursuit to gather pieces of his other victims. The bone harp grew with each delay. By the time I reached the place where the river joined the sea, the instrument was nearly as tall as a woman, yet I stood as straight as ever as I cradled those silenced girls, my sister at the center.

The townspeople waved flags and shouted praise on the streets, yet fear lurked behind drawn curtains protecting vulnerable daughters. The city held its breath, waiting for the prince to complete his business and return to his mountain kingdom, sacrificial bride in tow.

As I neared the city center, the braided strings began to quiver. The crowd parted to let me pass. I followed the bridal procession across the bruised and tattered petals that blanketed the cobbled streets and steps leading up to the cathedral. Incensed and outraged, the bone harp exhaled a flurry of notes. No one dared to stop me. White-faced attendants bowed their heads and opened the sealed chapel doors.

The prince paused in the act of lifting the bride's veil. A shadow passed over his face when he saw me standing in the aisle, a dark force cradling a harp built from the trail of broken bodies left in his wake. I pushed the cloak from my shoulders. Twyla's silver bells rang bright and true before falling silent once more.

A tangled murmuration of dead girls' cries swooped into that silence, and my sister's voice emerged as clear as the water in our old mill pond. Tywla took up the harper's tune, twisted the telling of truth.

'O yonder stands the prince, the would-be king,
Binnorie, O Binnorie;
There stands the prince who murdered me;
along the way to the mill-dam o' Binnorie.

Twyla cursed him, forced him follow. The prince ground his teeth, rolled his eyes, fought the compulsion with all his might, yet still he trailed us out of the church, through the streets, and down to the muddy riverbank.

Along the way, other voices rose from the bone harp, each verse a tribute to the lives torn asunder and then cast aside. Not a single person moved to bar our progress—not the bride in her gown of white, not the soldiers in their metal suits, not the townspeople in their colorful finery.

He chased me, forced me off the bridge,
Binnorie, O Binnorie.

The notes went higher and higher still. The prince cried out in terror or rage, not that it mattered. The bone harp trembled violently, forcing him to his knees. Up to his waist in the running water, the prince's fate belonged to me. Satisfied, a single note sounded, and the instrument broke apart, transformed into a flurry of starlings that rose to the sky.

But my arms were not empty for long.

I folded the would-be king into my deadly embrace and hummed the ballad's final refrain:

The prince's bones will break that dam;
Binnorie, O Binnorie.

GAZE WITH UNDIMMED EYES AND THE WORLD DROPS DEAD

With the temperature hovering just below zero and the hotel grounds buried hip deep in snow, I spent my first evening in the small Colorado town at the lobby bar. Dark, sticky wood kissed my elbows and the slightly sour scent of rotting fruit burrowed deep in my throat. Rocky Mountain National Park during high season might be a tourist's playground, but I was no tourist, and it sure as shit wasn't summer. Even winters in Anchorage had been warmer.

"Well, what do we have here," says a man's voice. "Hello, dollface."

I caught a glimpse of red plaid and a bushy beard before I averted my eyes. The comment was obviously aimed at me because the only one other customer sat at the end of the bar, and that old coot was firmly engaged with the sports feed rolling across a flat screen. The TV tilted in a haphazard way just above a makeshift wine rack. Suspended from their stems, the upside-down goblets were furred with dust. There was more than one reason I preferred whiskey over wine. I ran my tongue over my teeth and shifted my weight on the barstool, presenting a back as stiff as a board to my would-be suitor.

Battered wooden legs protested as the man pulled out an empty stool to encompass his broad frame. The bartender slid a brimming, wide-mouth tumbler across the bar. Out of the corner of my eye, I watched the stranger shoot the amber liquid as though it was sugared water, not 80 proof.

"Another," he said. "One for the lady, too."

I decided to ignore him and stabbed at the candied cherries lurking under layers of ice and whiskey at the bottom of my Old-Fashioned. A note chimed as though I'd stirred the clapper of a small silver bell. I frowned and jabbed again. One of the cherries broke free from the others. It rose at my prodding, a beady eye emerging from the amber liquid, a black imitation of life's spark hidden behind the lens.

I gasped and pushed away from the bar, nearly toppling in my haste to stand up. The glass eye jittered in my drink, clinking against melting ice as it struggled to stay afloat. It spun drunkenly, bobbing along until its weight pulled the glass sphere back under. As if that wasn't shocking enough, another black orb plopped out of nowhere to join it.

"What the fuck!"

I pushed back from the bar and shifted to stand.

The man sitting next to me laughed a deep rumbling sound like a bear. "You got the lucky seat." He pointed to a weasel-like creature chained to the ceiling right above my spot at the bar. "That's Lucky. He loses those damn eyes of his maybe two, three times a week."

The critter's fur bristled in warning, skin awkwardly bunched as though there hadn't been enough weasel to cover the taxidermy form. I should have found relief in the cobwebs stretching between tattered ears, but the way the fur splintered around the empty eyeholes left me dizzy and unmoored.

"Excuse me," I said. A reflex response.

"I don't think he minds much." The man in red plaid chortled. "I know *I* don't. Means I can buy you a *proper* drink."

He leaned over and fished the taxidermy eyeballs out of my glass. He prodded the wooden screws with a serrated spoon. The handle looked ridiculously small between his fingers.

"The eye sees a thing more clearly in dreams than the imagination awake," he said.

"What?"

The man wrapped the glass eyes in a handkerchief and stowed the bundle away in his flannel's breast pocket. "Leonardo da Vinci." He polished the spoon on his sleeve and slipped it next to the folded-up kerchief.

He waved a hand at the barkeep, who removed the remains of the ruined drink and replaced it with two dull glasses and a fresh bottle of high-end scotch. Scotch, not whiskey. I couldn't abide the stuff.

"No, thanks." I gathered my purse and fumbled for my room key. "I was just leaving."

The man stopped me with a hand roughened by hard weather. "I insist."

I froze, trapped by his touch. But before I could react, he released me and uncorked the single malt. His callused fingers stroked the bottle as though it was a living thing. In spite of myself, I felt a thrill at the chase. It had been a while since I'd been the object of a man's desire.

"You'll love this." The scent of peat and smoke unfurled, as he poured.

He nudged a glass towards me and picked up the other. He tilted the tumbler and paused expectantly.

What did I really have waiting in my hotel room anyway? The tavern might not have many amenities, but it did feature a big, brick fireplace that shed warmth. My allotted lodging for the night was cold, decked out in the impersonal white linen expected in even the shoddiest of lodges. I hated white. I hated the cold. So, I slid back into my seat.

"Just one." I clinked his glass with my own. The sound echoed for a moment like a trap springing in the snow, and I winked up at Lucky. *Who's lucky now?* The scotch burned all the way down.

I loosened up a little after that first measure. My companion kept my glass full, as he told me tales of the Colorado wilderness and the animals that lived there. With a glint in his eye, he talked about the demons that roamed on four legs through the woods, devils that hid in the guise of simple animals.

"You can tell them from normal critters by the traps they lay for people." He wagged his fingers and began counting off the predators, one by one. "Bears, lynx, cougars, wolves, foxes."

I thought he looked like a bear and told him so. He laughed again. I held out the tumbler, eager to switch the conversation. Anything to keep from discussing foxes. Anything to soften the sharpness lodged like claws in my spine.

It worked too. A little while later, the combined heat of the fire and the scotch made me desperate for cool sheets. My new friend helped me down the maze of long halls patterned with a faded floral pattern that looked more like animal entrails than elegant vines. The white doors seemed to stretch on forever. The bearded man at my side kept me upright, and I leaned into his strength. He might have told me his name, or maybe not. I didn't care. First names were slippery devils. I called everyone "darling." Much easier all the way around.

That night, I dreamed I was back in Alaska. A span of a year I preferred to avoid thinking about during the day. But at night, the eye does indeed see things in dreams more easily suppressed in the waking hours. I remembered the full-length fox coat I'd coveted juxtaposed against the gritty reality of a vixen choked in a snare glittering against the snow. I remembered the sound of the creature's claws scrabbling on the tail gate when it regained consciousness. I remembered the wet thud of an empty wine bottle connecting with flesh and fur. My ex had only smiled when I told him I'd changed my mind. *You'll love it*, he'd said with arrogant confidence, *wait and see.*

Sometime last night, when I'd laughed about the stranger's stories of evil bears and malicious foxes, he'd said the same thing. *Wait and see.*

I woke up in a foul mood with a fouler mouth. After a couple of nightcaps, I had the habit of forgetting to brush my teeth before passing out. And last night, I'd lost count after four. Or was it five? Absently, I ran my tongue over furred enamel. The feeling that I was forgetting something gnawed at the jagged edges of a hangover, but I pushed the uneasiness aside. I reached for the tumbler of water I always kept near the bed, but my groping hand encountered something unfamiliar, something that shifted at my touch.

Sleeping mask hastily shoved aside, I gaped at a mound of marbles stacked on the nightstand. Not marbles, eyes. They gleamed in various shades of gold, brown, and black. The pupils set deep within each of the glass orbs watched me, as I scrambled backward, nearly toppling off the far side of the bed in my haste to escape their judgment. The carpet crunched under my weight. Bits and pieces of wood and dried moss had been scattered across the floor. Someone, *something* had been in my room while I slept. I couldn't catch my breath, so I just stood there counting seconds with each inhalation.

The phone rang, a shrieking sound oddly reminiscent of a fox sounding an alarm. As if in response, the pyramid of eyes shuddered and then collapsed in a clatter of glass bouncing against glass. I didn't answer the call, didn't have to. A quick check of the vivid orange numbers glaring from the clock told me everything I needed to know. My first day on the job and I'd overslept.

I did my best to ignore the bark and moss and eyes, focusing instead on getting my ass out the door in hopes I would be able to keep my position. By the time I made it down two flights of well-worn stairs and a long white corridor flooded with fluorescent lights, my headache had reached epic proportions. Pre-made excuses sprinted for the finish line, as I slipped into the boardroom. Migraine. Stomach flu. Power outage. Suicidal friend. Dying parent. They rolled and tumbled over each other in a mad rush to win the day. But my false smile slipped when I realized only one person was waiting for me on the other side of the door. Worse yet, I knew the man. The stranger from the tavern. He was wearing jeans and the same red flannel I'd pressed my face against last night in the hall. I was intimately aware of the nip marks scattered across my skin and tenderness between my legs.

"What are you doing here?"

The bearded man leaned back in chair and looked me over, from head to toe.

"Feeling a little rough, Ms. Kingston?" The chair tipped back on all fours. The man poured a healthy measure of French roast from a coffee carafe and gestured to the chair on his left. "Have a seat."

Little details clicked into place. My questions about the pile of glass eyes and the mud-stains on the bedroom carpet slipped away with the sudden realization of who I was facing. "You're Bruce Boston." Was he grinning under that thick beard? Of course, he was. "This is your hotel."

"I had my staff let you sleep in this morning. I figure you needed your rest."

Smug shitbird. Two could play that game. "So, kind of you," I said, adding a little Southern drawl to the vowels for added emphasis.

I slid into my assigned seat. "What's on the agenda today, boss?"

"Cream or sugar?" he asked, polite. Distant.

"No cream." I used a pair of delicate silver prongs to count out five sugar cubes. Bruce didn't say anything, so I added a sixth just for the hell of it. "Do you have a spoon?"

He pulled the serrated spoon out of his breast pocket and slid it to me across the table. I made an attempt at nonchalance, as I stirred the dissolving sugar cubes, click-clacking the silver against the rim while trying not to think of glass eyes.

"We'll start with a tour of the hotel and then finish up with a review of your duties."

I bristled. If he thought I was going to add sexual favors to my list of *duties*, mister man had another thing coming. "I'm well aware of your expectations, Mr. Boston. I already signed the contract at the agency."

"Humor me," he said. "Tomorrow is soon enough to introduce you to the rest of the staff. When you're feeling better."

He stood up, and I followed him, cup in hand. When he wasn't looking, I slipped the silver spoon into my hip pocket.

The original hotel had been added on to multiple times over the last fifty years. The result was a twisted maze of hallways and levels. In some places the seams of the floors didn't meet, resulting in a whole series of strange staircases and ramps. Even without a hangover, I strongly doubted I could find my way back to the lobby without directions.

Bruce didn't seem to mind the long hallways and ghastly floor coverings, but the fluorescent lights and twisting patterns made it difficult to keep my coffee down. Stuffed animals were everywhere— the ballrooms, tavern, tearoom, dining room, lobby, conference rooms, and even in the enclosure dedicated to an indoor pool. The critters looked even older and more mismatched than the hotel. And they watched everything. By the time we made it back to the boardroom, I was trying to figure the easiest way out of my contract. Management position and full benefits be damned.

Grateful to be off my feet, I settled into my abandoned chair and wondered if I should attempt another cup of coffee on a sour stomach.

"Any chance of getting tea instead?" I asked.

My would-be-employer nodded and picked up the receiver of an old-fashioned phone. I took the moment to take a better look at my surroundings. Wood paneling covered the walls, a gleaming golden expanse broken only by inset bookcases at either end. Books that appeared to have been selected and sorted by the color of their covers filled the shelves and, in one corner, a ratty stuffed beaver hunched over a branch on the uppermost shelf. It took a minute before I realized the creature was watching with hollow eyes. Just like Lucky.

Bruce placed an order for a tea service. Just as he hung up, a loud clattering rattled down the fireplace. A glass eye, larger than a silver dollar, dropped from the chimney and into the fireplace where the wooden screw attached to the glass sparked in the hot coals.

Bruce leaned against the credenza. "Interesting."

"Interesting? Are you serious? What the actual fuck?'

Its companion rattled the metal on its way down before plopping in the flame next to its twin. I thought of my dreams and the look of that damned fox back in Alaska. Those eyes had been amber, not black like Lucky's. Had there been a glint of amber in the glass spheres stacked near the bed? I couldn't remember.

"Are we done here? I think I need to lie down."

My new employer rewarded me with a curt nod. "A word of advice, Ms. Kingston." He glanced at the fireplace and then back at me. "Don't go wandering off. The woods can be dangerous in winter."

"I have no plans to go hiking, Mr. Boston." I stood up abruptly, irritable and ill all at once. "Good day."

But once I was out in the hall, I realized I had no intention of going back to my room. What if the glass eyes were still there, or worse, what if they were gone? I crept from room to room, taking the long hallways from one side of the hotel to the other in search of absolution. Wherever I roamed, there were dozens of taxidermy animals waiting for me. I found everything from squirrels to bears, but one creature, in particular, eluded me. I moved my search to the other buildings on the property.

Outside, everything became clearer. My breath escaped in little clouds. The cold cut through my clothes, and I couldn't help but wonder how much warmer I would have been in the fox coat I'd been promised. The snow blazed in the bright light. Paths had been carved from door to door. In other places, the snowpack revealed tracks—the swooping half circles of a rabbit loping, long scratches cut from a bird hopping from one tree to the next, the deep paw prints of a predator stalking its prey.

It had been a day just like this one when my ex had found the fox caught in the snare. Up until that point, I'd never seen a fox in the wild, but there it had been, red fur shining like a stain on the snow. I remembered looking the other way. There was nothing I could have done, I'd told myself, even though I knew it was a lie.

But that had been years ago. That trapped fox had never been skinned. My ex had let the carcass freeze under the covered truck bed where it had stayed all winter. I'd only looked at the dead beast once, just before I left Alaska for good. The dead fox stared back. It still watched me in my dreams, but maybe that wasn't enough anymore.

In winter, the sun sets early in the north. That baleful eye cast an orange-tinted glow on the snowbanks. Black tree limbs stretched like a fence separating the hotel grounds from the forest beyond. And animals, surely more than I could imagine, paced that line between my world and theirs. Did they lament for their brethren, those brittle, faded sections of skin and fur clinging hopelessly to wooden forms? Did they see us living our hostile lives through the glass lens screwed into the eye sockets of those taxidermy animals? I wasn't sure.

I walked a little farther, pushing out along a trampled path only wide enough for one person to pass. It led away from the shoveled walks into the wilder places, drawing closer to the bleak forest beyond. I felt more like I was wading than walking, but I persisted. Just a few more steps and I'd turn back. The fresh air would do me good. Although I couldn't see bird nor beast, I felt certain they watched me from the screen of black tree limbs menacingly tangled at the edge of civilization.

A crow screamed. The rasping caw was taken up by dozens, if not hundreds of other black-winged voices. I stopped and covered my ears as I searched the trees for a murder. I should be able to see them, shouldn't I? Or was it possible that I couldn't see the birds in the trees, the beasts slipping through the underbrush, because my eyes were not my own?

The sun dipped a little lower, its light partially obscured by the trees. The amber glow deepened. Frantically, I looked around. Snow and cold surrounded me. The only hint of civilization was a section of the hotel roof I could see in the distance behind me. Everywhere else, the snow shimmered like a mirror cobbled together from millions of fragments of silvered glass. That's when I heard the delicate sounds of approach, a furred song played from the contact of swift feet on frost.

A blaze of red and white crested the snow-covered slope just off to the side of the path. The vixen stopped and stared, the dark empty sockets accusing the damned.

"It's not my fault," I protested.

The fox grinned, her teeth sharp as filed accusations.

I slipped a hand into my pockets and wrapped numb fingers around the handle of the silver spoon. It was small, but precise.

"I couldn't do anything to stop it," I said, one last attempt.

The fox opened its mouth and laughed.

The crows joined her in a raucous display, taking wing by the hundreds in a billowing cloud of feathers. Did those birds have eyes, or had they been replaced with glass too? I couldn't tell. I couldn't feel my arms or feet. The cold chewed on my face and nibbled on my bones. No fur coat for me. Not now, not ever. The fox moved closer, mouth agape, as I lifted the spoon. My eyes weren't black like a crow's or gold like that of a fox, but they worked just fine and that would have to do.

CRACKED

Helen stayed stoic throughout her labor, but when the doctor finally settled a large egg on her stomach instead of the red-faced, squalling infant she'd been expecting, her composure finally broke. It began with tears and escalated into hysterical laughter. The attending nurse, an old battle-axe, gave her a reproachful look and muttered something about first-time, middle-aged mothers before whisking the egg to safety. After a few minutes Helen's laughter shifted back to sobs, which eventually wound down to a desultory silence.

She had prepared for a natural delivery. After Dan left, she instead opted for an epidural. The anesthesiologist told her she was fine, but Helen insisted she was having some sort of weird reaction to the pain medications. She sulked in her bed, as the nurses cooed over the "little darling" in the bassinet. No one told her how brave she was. No one marveled over her impossible delivery of a ten-pound *egg*. In fact, no one gave her any attention at all.

At the nurses' insistence Helen forced herself to hold the swaddled bundle, but she immediately deposited it back into the bassinet as soon as they left. Each time she handled the smooth shell, she remembered the damn "egg baby" assignment she'd failed in junior high home economics. Back then, she only had to care for a hollowed-out chicken egg. But after she crushed the second one in less than an hour, the teacher gave her a "flour baby" to take care of instead. At the end of the unit, she turned in a plate of chewy brownies wrapped in an empty flour sack. The teacher wasn't amused. Helen took that lesson to heart: babies will ruin your life, not to mention your GPA.

A nurse half her age came into the room with discharge papers. She was dressed in seasonally pastel scrubs decorated with pink bunnies and colored eggs, her identification badge covered with snapshots of bright-eyed toddlers. Helen glanced from those pictures to the massive egg propped up in the beige car carrier. Maybe Dan hadn't been the father after all. Maybe some kinky Greek god had visited her in the guise of a bird. Not that she'd willingly fuck a bird. Would she? Thinking about it made Helen's head hurt.

"It's hard work, especially for a woman your age." The young nurse winked knowingly, as she snapped pink gum between even white teeth. "Do you have a name picked out?"

Helen bristled. Of course, she had names picked out. She was a logical woman who worked with numbers and charts on a daily basis. But there was nothing normal about her current situation. The names she'd selected all had specific meanings. She had one for a girl and one for a boy and even had a second of each just in case twins showed up. Surprises happen, right? But none of those carefully collated monikers would work for an *egg*. What were the alternatives? Shelby? Egbert? Benedict? The whole situation was ridiculous.

She finally settled on Pascal, a nod to her favorite philosopher-mathematician, but left the box denoting the father blank. When she got home, Helen took Pascal straight to the nursery she'd so painstakingly decorated in neutral shades of cream and tan. The understated, yet elegant toile wallpaper featured characters from the classic Mother Goose nursery rhymes—Humpty Dumpty was, of course, included.

Helen sighed and lowered Pascal into the crib. The smooth shell gleamed.

She decided to change the nursery's theme to something bold and bright, dinosaurs perhaps. With that, she kissed Pascal good night and turned out the lights.

Over the next few days, Helen rigorously researched everything she could find on how to hatch eggs. She discovered that the largest eggs on land came from ostriches, but Pascal's size broke all records. The horrifying discovery led to a whiskey-fueled inspection of her lady bits in a hand mirror. Whether it was the booze or the low lighting, the damage wasn't as extensive as she'd feared. Even so, Helen decided Pascal would just have to deal with being an only child.

Stable in the career she'd built over two decades, Helen decided to continue her work as a tax accountant from home. The regular pedicures, injections, and salon visits resumed; however, this time she had the stylists come to her. And, although she never experienced a rush of maternal love, Helen excelled at caring for Pascal's physical needs just as she excelled at each endeavor she undertook.

In her off-hours Helen began to redecorate the nursery. Unwilling to deal with the mess and hassle of living plants, she draped green silk tacked to the ceiling. For a bit of added flair, she pinned on dozens of fabric leaves—quilted maple, beaded aspen, embroidered palm. The baby swing and changing table she replaced with large stuffed dinosaurs custom ordered to match the blue-green leaves and orange blooms in the jungle-themed curtains. The crib she dismantled as well. In its place, she pieced together designer pillows and sheets to form a nest large enough for her to rest comfortably. Whenever she began to feel broody, she'd climb in and curl up with Pascal, basking in the warmth of the grow lights hanging in every corner.

The egg still hadn't hatched after forty-five days. And that's when Helen decided they both needed some fresh air. She used organic makeup to create a face for Pascal. The eyes were lopsided, but adorable in their own way. She tucked the swaddled egg into the new stroller she'd modified with a portable heating blanket. After a quick touch-up with a lipstick pencil and a swipe of gloss, Pascal was deemed presentable and off they went.

Two houses away, a woman blocked their path on the sidewalk. She was dressed in stained clothing and cradled a bulging sling tied across her chest.

"Make-up on a baby?" the stranger gasped. "What kind of monster are you?"

The question startled Helen, who'd been minding her own business, thinking about the potential of natural dyes to give Pascal a more sophisticated look.

Helen wrinkled her nose at the disheveled and obviously distraught young woman. Even from the distance of a few feet, there was a strong smell of talcum powder, sour milk, and urine. Totally unprovoked, a baby began to cry, a loud whooping wail. The sling distorted, as the creature inside struggled for immediate attention. Horrified, Helen took advantage of the distraction and continued on her way, prim heels clicking against the sidewalk. As she rounded the corner, she shook her head in disgust.

Some women just weren't meant to be mothers.

AN EMBRACE OF POISONOUS INTENT

No one had died *yet*, but they would. Every human life, from the city gates to the castle towers, would be extinguished before the week was out—with one exception. That is, everyone would die unless *she* came, and I knew my lover wouldn't fail me now.

I stood on the balcony, shrouded in shadow. In the courtyard below, physicians and witches alike came and went. The source of the illness had finally been traced to the town's sole water supply, filtered clear and pure through the stones of the mountain surrounding the fortress. No one had ever considered the possibility that it could have been tainted, that the great Illys Mal would fall, defeated by an invisible threat—until now.

A knock on the door woke the cockatrice curled at my feet. Its feathers rustled under the draping of my gown. The creature crowed like a rooster at dawn when the door creaked open.

"Forgive me, your Grace."

My manservant slid through the crack. Mirrored glasses obscured his eyes, but his body language told me all I needed to know. A pity. I appreciated loyalty above all else, but fidelity was no antidote to what plagued him.

"There is nothing to forgive, Elric." Sometimes half-truths are necessary to maintain balance.

"Messages have been sent by bird. The drums sounded, fires lit." He paused and clenched his fists at his sides as the cockatrice pushed the fabric aside to peek out from the confines of my skirt.

"But?"

"There's still no sign of help."

Bells rang and rang and rang. The infernal din frayed my nerves. The good people of Illys Mal had been protected so long they no longer knew how to react to such an intimate threat.

"All the gates have been sealed?"

"Yes, your Grace." He opened a hand to reveal the king's key. "No one can leave or enter without your permission."

You will save me, won't you? Elric questioned—an unspoken plea, but heard nonetheless.

I swept forward, enjoying the way the silk dress rustled as I moved. It had been dyed a twilight blue edging on purple. Many people had perished to create this signature color, and none dared to wear it but me. Even processed, the color carried the taint of shells crushed to create it. Anyone who touched it without immunization would linger in agony before eventually succumbing to death.

Elric flinched but did not move when I plucked the key from his palm with a gloved hand. I rewarded him with a slight smile. The port stain that dappled his jaw darkened. The cockatrice flapped its ungainly wings and squawked in protest at being left behind. Its scaly tail scraped against the floor as it followed.

"I'm going down to work in the garden." I slipped the key into a hidden pocket sewn into my skirt. It settled, rustling the dried petals I kept with me at all times. The fragrance of long-dead silver blossoms perfumed the air around me. "See to it that the marked crates in my workroom are brought to me."

Hurry, Saēna. I scooped the cockatrice into my arms and braced myself to appear in control as I walked through the castle corridors of the dead king, my late husband. *Hurry, before it's too late.*

***

We first met, she and I, under the canopy of silent silver. The translucent flowers rained their glittery pollen at the slightest touch. Saēna huddled at the base of the tree. Her bared shoulders gleamed under the streaks of moonlight shining through the glass-like petals. If not for her weeping and the dishevelment of her clothes, I might have mistaken her for a fairy.

I'd come prepared to gather pearled berries ripened under the full moon. Like many of the most beautiful poisons in the world, the silent silver tree had properties that also healed. Those were of no interest to me. I didn't think they were of importance to Saēna either—at least not then. Only the most promising poisoners were allowed to train with the grey sisters, and I was the brightest of them all. I placed the blonde as a new recruit, but that didn't explain her presence in the most lethal of all the world's gardens sitting under the heavy boughs of one of the most dangerous trees in existence.

"What are you doing here?" I asked, not quite able to take the bite out of the inquiry.

I'd been told more than once that my speaking voice was as sharp as stinging nettles. It came from keeping to myself, I suppose. But, when I saw her sitting there, I couldn't help but break my vows. Her presence stripped away all my desire for solitude. I loved her immediately, and there was nothing I could do but fall to my knees at her side.

The girl didn't flinch like others did when they saw the scars on my face. Perhaps the moon hid them for once, but I doubted it.

"It reminds me of home," she said in a voice as sweet as mine was bitter.

Impossible, of course. The legendary island that was the birthplace of silent silver trees had sunk beneath the waves and never reemerged. There had been no survivors. She was not a novice of the order then, but a madwoman locked away in the beauty of her youth. A shame.

I felt compelled to reason with the girl even though others had surely done the same—and failed.

"Nimuēh Úll drowned long ago."

"I know," she said with a sigh of longing that made me quiver.

Although I was forbidden by sacred vows to touch another woman in the heat of lust, I placed a hand on her shoulder. The coolness of her moon-touched skin made me feel as though I was on fire. And perhaps I was. I marveled at the effect she had on me. Only she was mad. And I had dedicated my life to developing the poisons the grey sisters used to rule the world.

She lifted her bowed head and turned to look at me with a face as round and pale as the moon. "I came to these shores wrapped in the embrace of silent silver. The tree saved me, lulled me to sleep. I dreamed." Her eyes swallowed the moon. "Why am I here?"

"You don't have to worry." I swept flower petals from her skin, the texture between the two indistinguishable. "No harm will come to you here."

"This place is full of death."

Before I could stop the girl, her hand darted forward as fast a minnow to touch the ribbon I wore tied around my throat. I shrieked, but it was too late. That unwarranted brush of skin against satin spelled doom. Unlike her, I'd spent years building up an immunity to the hazardous dye that stained the ribbon a deep indigo. Anyone else who came in contact would succumb to paralysis and, eventually, death. It was a secret formula that belonged to me alone, a dye concocted from a rare mollusk that roamed the sea floor.

"I slept a long time," the girl explained somberly. "The ocean and its inhabitants are old friends."

I ignored her claim and waited for her to succumb to the toxins. Although I hadn't cried in more than two decades, tears ran freely down my cheeks. No antidote existed, yet she didn't fall over in a stupor. She didn't froth at the mouth like a rabid animal. She didn't do anything but watch me weeping for her. The minutes stretched on, and I began to hope. Eventually, false dawn tinted the horizon pink. The girl gathered her skirt in a makeshift apron filled with petals and berries gifted by the silent silver.

"My name is Saēna," she said.

I followed, ignoring the ache in my lower back and knees as I stood up. Saēna looked up at the tree, the leaves still glowing from the last of the moonlight. Her lips parted as though she was waiting for a drink that would cure her of all ills. I couldn't resist the drive of desire a moment longer.

"Achlys." I muttered my own name against the curve of her lips. She opened her mouth under the pressure of my tongue.

She twisted her shoulders and slipped free from the simple dress. Flowers and fabric spilled around her bare feet. Saēna pulled me back down to the ground, and I followed willingly.

"Achlys," she whispered. "Dream with me."

And I did. Goddess help me, I did.

***

Like the fortified mountain city Illys Mal, there was only one way in and out of the queen's garden. Under the guidance of my hand, it had been transformed from the stuffy formal space I first entered a decade earlier to a wild and poisonous garden that had no equal in all the known world. Not even the half-remembered garden of the grey sisters could compare. In all ways but one, the enclosed plot contained everything I needed for the continuation of my craft. Despite the altitude and bright sun, I'd even been able to coax a silent silver from seed to tree although it had yet to produce fruit of its own. There was still time for the tree, for it was young even though I was not. I knew that with enough patience, all things would surrender to fruition.

The cockatrice warbled with venomous insistence as it struggled to keep up with me. It stepped on the trail of my skirt and tangled in the material. Finally, I relented and scooped the creature up.

"I wish you'd make up your mind." The miniature monster rumbled contentedly in the crook of my arm. "Don't worry. You should be able to practice your talents soon enough."

Even though the cockatrice was the favorite of my brood of venomous creatures, I hadn't bothered to name it. For my purposes, it was as useful as any plant in my garden—a tool. Besides, names came with attachment, and I'd long since turned away from those inclinations. My work was my life. I'd become stronger and more deadly than any poisoner who had come before and any who might follow after. Thousands had perished at my hands, and many more would suffer before my work was complete.

I glanced at the cloudless blue sky trapped by the jagged teeth of the mountains. The sun stood nearly overhead—its brightness intense in ways I'd never become accustomed to. I preferred lowland territories where there was suitable cover from the elements. High in the alpine valley everything felt exposed and thin. All of which made it the perfect place to set a trap.

I settled to wait for my guest on the sun-warmed stone bench near the central fountain. Clear water trickled down the patinaed curves of a feminine figure balanced on a branch. Glass-like leaves from the silent silver floated in the water. The cockatrice jumped from my embrace to terrorize a line of death watch beetles marching along the pool's edge. Its antics amused me, yet the minutes still dragged on. Patience was a virtue of mine, but even I could only bear so much.

The bells doggedly continued to announce the doom already inside the town's bolted doors. If only they would stop. No one could escape the effects of the tainted water. It was inevitable. Hence, the infernal bells and the frantic scuffle of people trying to find a way out. Fools.

The cockatrice spread its wings, craned its neck, and hissed. A shadow consumed the sun as an enormous avian figure glided across the high mountain valley. It was so large it could have easily lifted a whale from the sea and carried it far away. The bird swooped down, silhouette rippling across the king's wall, the bell towers, the castle garden. It settled for a moment, suspended over the central fountain where I waited. Even though I shaded my eyes, I couldn't see if it carried passengers or not. But I knew. Oh, how I knew.

There'd been a time, early on, when Saēna willingly joined me in the delicate dance between life and death. She trained at my side. Later, she trailed me from city to city, healing that which I'd compromised. I was easy on her at first, and I employed the same poisons I'd devised in her presence. The antidotes were formulas known only to her. She followed me from river valleys to sandstone mesas astride a griffin's back. I had yet to create a poison she could not defeat, yet still the casualties piled up. She might have become the greatest healer in the world, but even she couldn't save everyone.

Backlit by the sun, the interior of the hovering beast was as dark as an inkblot. Around the edges of the massive wings, fiery feathers glinted. I had suspicions about the creature's origin. Between scented sheets, Saēna had told me tales about Nimuēh Úll, tales of priestesses who danced with trees, tales of monsters born from the depths of the earth, tales of seduction and betrayal and love.

The bird screamed—a sound more suited to a grief-stricken woman than a monster with flight feathers longer than I was tall. Yet, I recognized the challenge. *Soon enough*, I promised myself as the beast flapped its massive wings, carrying my lover to the top of the tallest tower of my long-dead husband's castle. So be it then.

The cockatrice grunted in satisfaction, certain in its power. If it had been any other occasion, I would have reinforced the behavior with a feast of sand scorpions. As it was, however, I needed to prepare for my guest.

The sound of boot heels scraping on stone announced the arrival of my faithful Elric. Loaded down with an assortment of carefully marked crates, a pair of indentured servants nervously followed him down the stone path leading to the center of the labyrinth where I sat. His usual aplomb set aside, Elric's face was so flushed from exertion the port stain was barely visible. His mirrored lens reflected the beauty of the spot I'd cultivated so carefully.

"She's here, your Majesty."

The poor man feared my wrath, the slaves even more so. But the contents of those boxes were more for show than anything. I didn't need special ingredients, complex potions, or venom-tipped weapons to defeat my love. I'd planned too carefully for that.

"Put them over there." I waved a hand at the clear space near the fountain.

The cockatrice ignored the approach of my subjects and dashed into the foxglove in pursuit of a vivid yellow, ruby-throated dart.

In his haste, Elric had neglected to provide even the smallest measure of protection for the men burdened down with gifts for my beloved. The cockatrice emerged from the tall fronds. The pink and purple flowers nodded, their brown speckled throats open as though they hungered for something just out of reach. The cockatrice jumped up next to me and dropped the dead dart in my lap. One of the men shouted in a language I'd never bothered to learn. Crates fell to the ground as he and his companion turned to flee.

I commanded the cockatrice to attack with a single word. The scaly beast flapped its leathery wings and launched itself after its quarry. The men shouted and tried to stay close to each other. Perhaps they thought a united front would offer some protection. But a cockatrice doesn't kill with iron-sharp talons or venom-infused fangs.

My pet landed in the middle of the only path leading out from the garden's spiraling center. The cockatrice flared its wings and warbled a demand for the men to look. One complied. His legs crumpled, and he fell face first into a border of wolfsbane. The other frantically closed his eyes and prayed to his dead god.

I stood. Elric bowed and stepped out of my way. The remaining man stood there chanting, his foreign green eyes firmly pressed shut. I grabbed his jaw with an ungloved hand and squeezed. He looked at me then. Oh, how he looked.

"Where do you think you're going?"

He was dead already, of course. No man could bear my touch and live. But I didn't stop my pet from climbing my skirts. In its eagerness to destroy, the cockatrice tore the silk as easily as a blade had once scored the skin on my cheeks, marking my rise in glory as a superior in the order of the grey sisters. Once the cockatrice reached my shoulder, the beast flared its wings and issued a cry that promised death. The man's eyes flared open, and he slumped to the ground. The monster glided down to land on the dead slave's chest. It crowed as proudly as any rooster.

"Clean this up." I said to Elric, as I bent to sort through the tumbled cases. "Immediately."

"Yes, your Majesty," said my manservant, yet he didn't move. He just stood there staring as the cockatrice tore out one of the slave's green eyes and gulped it down as easily as a snake swallows an egg.

"There are worse ways to die." I reminded him as I paused in my sorting.

Elric avoided interrupting the cockatrice in its snack. Instead, he grabbed the ankles of the other man face down in the blue blooms and dragged him back down the path they'd come. He returned shortly for the other casualty. I ignored the soft thump of the man's hollow face hitting the paving stones as Elric dragged him away.

I had more important things to think about than servants and slaves.

Saēna and I had things to discuss.

***

Although there had been a hundred little hints over the course of our first few years together, I'd been able to deny Saēna's attraction to antidotes—for the most part. She willingly processed poisons at my side, but then refused to employ them. And, if I didn't watch her carefully, my subjects often survived despite my best efforts. Yet she was mine, as surely as I was hers. I refused to believe she'd ever betray me.

And then I found her under the silent silver with a unicorn's head nestled in her lap. The creature fled when I revealed myself.

"What have you done?" I grabbed her by her shoulders and pulled her to her feet.

The grey sisters' determination to limit the supply of unicorn horns meant the creatures were nearly extinct. There hadn't been a sighting in years and, even then, rumors of the maned beast had come from a kingdom far in the north near the Crown of the World. The grey sisters would surely destroy Saēna if they discovered her communing with the woodland creature. One touch of a unicorn's horn and a poisoned well could be purified. That was not a power to be taken lightly.

"Tell me you lured it here in order to kill it," I demanded.

"My love." Saēna pressed her palms against my scarred cheeks. The silent silver shuddered as she sighed. "I can do no such thing."

"This never happened. Do you hear me?" I shook her by her shoulders, and her hands fell from my face. "And it will never happen again. I forbid it."

"What are you afraid of?"

I released her and took a deep breath to steady my hand. I'd sworn an oath to the grey sisters, but I'd broken oaths before.

"Achlys?"

There was only one thing I was afraid of losing, and she seemed immune to my desire, and my fear.

I left her there in the garden. I couldn't bear her beauty, her innocence, her pure intention a moment longer. It wasn't until much later that I returned to harvest a living seed from the heart of the silent silver. I was still haunted by the image of the splintered stump near that broken fountain even though the fire had destroyed the cloister and all its gardens long ago. The grey sisters would never catch my bride. They would never break her on their altar. They would never destroy her beauty. The grey sisters were all dead, poisoned by one of their own.

Only I remained.

***

When the foreign girl found me, I realized Elric had finally given up hope that I'd save him. By then, I was used to betrayal, but it still stung.

"Did you kill him?"

The girl was a mere shadow of my beloved. I'd faced many of Saēna's acolytes over the years. Each and every one a flawed mirror of herself. None of them ever looked like me.

"We aren't murderers." The girl's spite was nearly as green as her eyes.

"But you didn't save him." Impatient, I peered around the girl. "Where is Saēna?"

The blonde nervously reached up to grasp at a ring tied around her throat with a silver ribbon. At the same moment, a streak of dark fur exploded out of the brush. The cockatrice spread its wings and turned to attack. But the animal didn't relent. Nor did it succumb to the cockatrice's deadly glare. Instead, it bared talons and teeth. Before I could react, the weasel had broken my favorite pet's neck. Feathers flew, and one of the cockatrice's wings snapped, bending at an odd angle.

"You would dare to enter my garden." I tore my gaze away from my cockatrice and its attacker. I would deal with the weasel later. "You dare to bring that *thing* into my presence. You dare to confront *me*?" I advanced.

The girl took a faltering step backwards. "In the name of all things holy, you cannot defeat me."

"She doesn't know you are here, does she?" The scars on my cheeks tugged under the force of a smile. "Saēna might not punish those who disobey her, but I will."

The girl may have fled then, but I was faster.

I caught her wrist, but she refused to release her grip on the ring. My ring. My promise to the one I loved. This girl had no right to wear it. She had no right to be in my presence at all and, for that, she would pay.

"I'm immune to your filthy touch." The girl's voice rose in panic. "I have been blessed by the Saint of Silent Silver."

She stabbed me with a dagger that she must have concealed in the folds of her robe. Her mouth opened in surprise when the blade bounced off the plating I always wore beneath the fabric of my dress. The grey sisters were masters of the poison arts, but we trained as warriors as well. Had Saēna forgotten so soon, or had she not bothered to train her own acolyte in the martial arts?

I snapped the girl's neck as easily as the weasel had defeated my cockatrice, only I was a hundred times more deadly. The girl's hunter attacked my ankles, but a sharp kick left it limp and broken on the paving stones. I tore the ribbon from the girl's throat and let the ring nestle in my open palm. Carved berries and leaves entwined along the silver surface. Which was I—the berries or the leaves? Which was Saēna? I'd thought we'd always be together. What were we, if not the twinned souls Fate ordained?

Saēna would come looking for the girl. Soon, she would be in my garden. She'd wear the ring that she'd so foolishly misplaced. And we would be together once more—as we were meant to be.

***

Saēna betrayed me a second time, but not with her unicorn. I'd hunted down the beast myself, sheared its silver mane and sawed off its horn while it was still alive. The unicorn wept like a woman right up until the moment I'd slit its throat.

Unicorns might be living antidotes to all known poisons, but my nature did not belong to this realm alone. Nor was I willing to accept defeat. If my bride could not help herself, if she was seduced by the purity of a unicorn's horn, then I would surround her with them until she became immune to the wild magic. I killed all that remained and, when I knew without doubt that the last unicorn had been exterminated from this world, I built a throne from their horns—the skull of that first betrayal set at the apex of the chair's high back.

When she saw my wedding gift, she did not weep or tear at her hair. Instead, she calmly took a seat on that hideous construction of horns—a queen in her own right.

"You should not tempt me so," Saēna said.

Fool that I was, I took this as a good sign. Our relationship would only grow stronger once she set aside her girlish notions. We would rule the world together, a world shaped by the subtlety of our craft.

I slipped the silver ring on her finger. The vines twisted. The leaves shivered. We were bound then and forever. Or so I thought.

Time moves oddly in my memories. Sometimes, it is as slow as a tree recording years, spreading its girth, ring after ring. Other times, it is as fast as quicksilver. A week, a month, a year later, I found Saēna once again under the shimmery leaves of the silent silver in the grey sisters' poison garden. She was not alone.

My bride sat astride a gryphon's back. The creature's feathers shone like hammered gold, its beak as sharp as sorrow. It stretched its wings, preparing to fly far away. I couldn't let that happen.

"Wait!" I frantically searched my pockets for a poisoned bolt, a shard of glass, anything to slow the beast down. "Saēna, wait. I beg you."

That caught her attention. She relaxed her grip on the ruff of fur where the lion's body meet the rill of feathers cresting the beast's head and shoulders. They both looked at me—her with eyes of silver, his with eyes of gold—and I knew I'd lost her already.

"You can't leave without me."

Even commoners knew the antidotal attributes of a griffin's claw, but the properties of the rest of the beast were uncharted territory. I was nearly as hungry for knowledge as I was for her. And, if there is one thing I'd learned from my beautiful bride, antidotes and poisons often exist side-by-side.

"Farewell, my love." She lifted a hand. Our wedding ring gleamed a coppery-red, a reflection from those cursed feathers.

The gryphon rose from the ground, its powerful wings creating a draft so vicious I was forced to cling to the fountain to stay on my feet. Whirlwinds of glass-like petals swirled in a mad frenzy, blinding me even as I struggled to watch my love leave me behind.

Once the draft died down and the beast was no larger than a sunspot, I unleashed my fury on the fountain. I vowed to dismantle it, stone by stone, poison the well, destroy the sisters, burn it all down. And then, only then, would I strip the silent silver down to its core to harvest a seed for a new hope, a new world. Saēna would return to me eventually, I promised myself.

She'd have to.

***

Over the years, I'd caught glimpses of my beloved from afar. She followed me from town to town, first on gryphon-back and later—once gryphons had been eradicated from the world—astride ground-bound beasts of burden. We passed decades in the flirtatious dance of curse and cure. I cultivated more and more elaborate poisons, extracted the deadliest venoms as I laid waste to region after region. Wherever I went, she followed, her silvery-blonde hair a pennant for peace and prosperity.

Saēna entered the queen's garden with the same sense of triumph and glory she possessed each time she saved what I had worked so hard to destroy.

"I wondered if you'd come." I pressed my palm against my cheek to stem the flush of blood rushing to betray me. My other hand clenched in a fist. "It's been so long."

She cocked her head as though assessing my worth. “Where you go, I follow.”

“And then you leave.” I couldn’t keep the bitterness out of my voice. “Again. And again.”

“Yes.” Saēna paused and bent down to check on her acolyte laying so very still across the stone path. She brushed the girl’s hair from her face, revealing purpled lips and bulging eyes. “You didn’t have to do that.”

I wasn’t sure if she was speaking to me or the acolyte.

Saēna stepped over the girl, not bothering to lift her silver skirts. The material soaked up the leftovers of death, leaving the hem rimmed an ugly yellowish red. She ignored me as well and went to the fountain where I’d lined up treasures collected from all the places we’d once passed through.

Her hand, pale as the moon, rested for a moment on the unicorn’s skull. The bone saw had left neat shear marks on the horn, which I’d severed with such delight all those years ago. She spent more time on the griffin claw that had been turned into a goblet studded with amethyst. There were other relics, too. A glass shoe from a town where sand pits were mined, the silicate melted and blown into imaginative vessels. A wheel of sharp cheese marbled with wine-stained veins. A jar of purple olives drenched in savory oil. A scarf dyed a green as deep as the dead acolyte’s eyes.

“I should have ended this long ago,” Saēna said, as though she could turn back time, bring back wild magic in its many forms.

“You’re here now.” *Finally.*

Saēna raised a hand. She was so close, but suddenly seemed farther away than ever. Where had she gone in the blank spaces of time during our dance of death? Where had she found the terrible beast that now acted as her steed? Why had she forsaken my love to save strangers? She was right in one thing. It needed to stop. We were meant to be together. I wouldn’t be denied any longer.

“You left me no choice.” I opened my fist to reveal the ring I’d given her on our wedding day. The circle had pressed deep into my palm.

The day grew dark as a shadow plunged into the sun. The enormous bird blocked the light. Time twisted. The stunted silent silver tree grew, spreading its branches in a twisted canopy above me. Buds emerged. Leaves unfurled. Berries pearled.

Saēna closed the distance between us. The silent silver rained pollen. My beloved unclasped her cloak, and I was taken back to the night I met her, this beautiful madwoman from the drowned city of Nimuēh Úll. A fey woman, a priestess who’d survived centuries cocooned in the loving embrace of a silent silver. Saēna's pale skin glistened as though she was the moon come to life.

"We all have a choice. It's a divine right." Saēna brushed her fingers across the scars on my cheeks. "You might be as fierce as a goddess but, in the end, you're mortal."

"Like you?" The words weighed as heavy on my tongue.

My beloved pulled me down to the carpet of petals scattered under the tree. I surrendered, unmindful of the press of roots reaching up through the loose soil to twine around me, around us.

"Achlys."

I shuddered at the sound of my name on her lips after decades apart. My mouth opened to hers, and I found myself drowning in a shadowy sea where bells still rang from the ocean floor, where broken gates opened and closed at the whim of ocean vents, where a silent silver towered higher than any castle turret and, in its uppermost branches, a bird burned as bright as lava erupting from the center of the world.

"Achlys," she whispered. "Dream with me."

And I did. Goddess help me, I did.

THE CERTAINTY OF SILENCE

The locksmith's eyes sparkle, but I cannot tell if he is smiling under the veil of coarse hair covering his cheeks, chin, and mouth. I reach up and brush my knuckles against the keys dangling from the thick mass. The newest one, tangled in a series of tightly woven braids, matches the silverwork of his other living bride's clockwork heart. He pushes my hand away.

"It doesn't belong to you." He kisses my forehead with lips that remind me of the succulent flesh torn from a living conch. "But soon you will have one of your very own."

The combined scent of ambergris and sandalwood perfume his beard. His skin smells like salt and sand and sun. I have changed over the last few months, but this man is the same as he was the day I allowed him to find me naked and crippled on his favorite stretch of beach. Curiosity that I am, I had no need for a voice to lure him to my side. He'd scooped me up and held me tight against his barrel chest. On the way to his seaside estate, he'd murmured promises and platitudes, never realizing I was the one who had chosen him.

He skims his hands across the cold length of my torso, fingers tracing the scars of my remaking. Tiny black stitches crisscross the concave hollow of my stomach. Mottled bruises ripple along the length of my newly formed waist. He nods and jots a few words down in a notebook before turning his attention to my useless lower limbs.

"Let me look at those lovely legs of yours," he says.

They are thick and clumsy. The dermis flakes off in patches, exposing windows of scaled skin streaked violet.

The cool metal of the table comforts me as he checks the mobility of my joints. His hands are hot and heavy against the cool dampness of my flesh. The keys, bound in the webbing of his beard, clank against the metal table and he bends closer to examine me. He probes between my legs with a fierce intensity, and for the first time I wonder how well he knew the woman who had provided these spare parts.

My chosen one dwarfs me in every way, but I am not afraid. Even when he wields the bone saws and shearing knives, his touch is gentle and light. I've survived worse tortures. I have lived in the deep dark places of the abyss beyond borders. I've been drowned, crushed, and mutilated. I've been broken and discarded. Through it all, I survived without ever uttering a single sound. My beautiful sister though, the winged siren who lured men to their deaths, that raven-haired temptress never learned the trick of it. Our father trapped her and dragged her to the bottom of the ocean to remind her of her duties. She screamed long after our father was finished with her. Some say she is screaming still.

In the corner, the meat lockers hum under the pressure of keeping the locksmith's collection of spare parts refrigerated and ready. The sound reminds me of the ocean's constant murmur urging me to return. Still, I hold my resolve.

He strips off my skin, layer after layer. The agony scours the hollows in my sinuses, and I struggle to breathe through the pain. The locksmith tells me that I am the only one of his brides who has never screamed; this appears to please him the way my silence also pleased my father. Everything fades to black when my intended starts breaking bones. The image of his blood-stained hands the last thing I remember.

When I wake, I am back in my case. No longer needed, the sea water that once filled the container has been drained. Yet, the thick wave of distortion in the glass calms me. It reminds me of home.

On the other side of the glass, the walls of the chamber are painted the pale blue of a robin's egg. Iron implements hang from the ceiling. Some of the devices shine with polished precision. Others are blackened and mottled with age. Russet flakes peel away from the metal bones, and bloody streaks mar the walls. With its low ceiling and curved walls, the chamber resembles a cave hidden at the bottom of the ocean. There are no windows and only the one door. A series of glass cases form a semi-circle around the operating table. The containers are tall but narrow, forcing me to bend my form in an unnatural way. Most of these prisons are occupied, but only two of us are still alive.

The other four brides are in various stages of decay, the causes of death evident in the various ways they had been cut apart and reassembled. Seen in order, they are a testament to the locksmith's evolving talents. The case farthest from where I'm kept contains a redhead who doesn't appear to have survived her first surgery. Her hands have been folded across a whittled-down waist. Thick copper hoops encircle exposed hip bones. The sections of skin left untouched sag from her frame like overheated wax.

The only other living bride is the locksmith's current obsession. No human should have been able to survive the series of operations our bridegroom has subjected her to. I wonder what ancient secrets live in her blood, where he found her. Even if I was able to voice those questions, she wouldn't be able to answer. The beribboned beauty never speaks, but when she cries, the pink heat of her open mouth is empty, stripped bare of teeth and tongue.

I ignore her and sit up to examine the locksmith's handiwork. I cannot see the color of my new legs under the livid bruises covering every inch of skin. The stippled pattern reminds me of the violet shading of my favorite fish. I close my eyes and concentrate on healing.

The girl in pink dies.

The locksmith goes into a vicious rage when he finds her. His curses remind me of my father on the day I found the bone flute and severed wings tucked away in his lair. I curl up in the corner of my case and wrap my arms around my new legs. The locksmith doesn't appear to notice me. All his attention is fixed on his dead bride, the newest in a collection of exquisite cadavers. He cuts a little silver key out of his beard and attempts to rewind her heart, but she remains limp and lifeless. He grabs her by her arms and shakes her, setting the silver rings around her neck clamoring like bells tolling for the dead. Finally, he relents. Head bowed, he carries her body out of the blue room.

The locksmith's distress brings a smile to my face. I know the girl in pink will return, but when she does it will be as a corpse bride. Soon, he will be forced to finish my remaking.

When the furious shading of my bruises fades from indigo and violet to a sickly chartreuse, the locksmith returns. The fifth bride is even more striking in death. Her polished silver rings and silky pink ribbons add definition to her delicate musculature. Her feet have been bound in matching satin, but the rest of her is left bare and beautiful. He installs hooks in the case and arranges her limbs so that she appears frozen in dance.

He leaves without looking at me.

The places where my skin has healed are the color of a sandy beach—a shifting array of topaz, citrine, and tiger's eye. If I look close enough, I can even see hints of volcanic glass in shades of obsidian and olivine. It's magnificent work, yet still it's not enough. I was the one who locked my voice away, but I do not have the key to releasing it. The locksmith can make a new key. He promised.

With my new feet and streamlined limbs, I pace the narrow confines of my prison, striking the glass with my palm at each turn. I am drowning, trapped, impatient with longing. I continue to pace. The dead girl in pink mocks me with her perfection, as I wait for my bridegroom to return. But when he does, he isn't alone.

If I hadn't already lost my voice, I would have lost it then. I am to become his masterpiece. He told me so himself. So why is she here, this new girl? I take my time looking at her, wondering if she is yet another wife or if he brought her here for spare parts.

At first glance, the young woman appears fragile, an angel bereft of wings. She is dressed in a white gown, but her arms and feet are bare. Her skin looks as though it's never seen the sun, and her eyes are as dark as secrets. Her hair, swept up in a twist, is as black as mine—a black so deep it's purple. The way she holds herself reminds me of my poor sister who was snared from the sky. Even when our father sheared the wings from her back, Leucosia remained defiant. This girl would be defiant, too. I almost pity her.

The locksmith settles her in the empty case and leaves without acknowledging me. Not spare parts, a wife then. I want to cry out, bring his attention back to me. I fear he will leave me unfinished. But I have no voice with which to scream. He dims the lights and leaves us in the dark with only the consistent hum of refrigeration to keep us company.

"Hello?" The new girl's voice sends shivers down my spine. "What's your name? What *is* this place?"

As if she doesn't know.

"My name is Maria," she offers.

A silence grows between us.

"What has he *done* to you?"

I want to tell her to save her pity for herself, but my words are locked in my throat. She continues with her questions, uncaring that I cannot or will not answer. I want to howl and scream and lament. I want to tear her apart and throw the pieces into to sea. Instead, I crouch in the corner and cover my ears with my hands while I wait for morning.

When the locksmith returns to the blue room, he comes straight to me. This time, when he takes me from my case, his touch is not gentle. His rage burns me. His lust bruises. The new girl hammers on the glass with her little white fists, as he straps me down on the operating table.

"Stop it. What are you doing to her?" The rapping of her knuckles becomes more frantic when he starts to peel away the golden webbing between my fingers. "Stop. Please stop!"

The locksmith opens my chest and begins the task of carving out a lifetime of darkness. Maria's screams become sobs. She splays her hands open; her pink palms press against the glass. Her eyes are wide and wet.

"I'm so sorry," she says.

I look away.

That night, Maria keeps me company. She tells me stories of her brothers and a life lived far from here. When she sings, it is nothing like a siren's song, but her lilting voice carries a magic of a different sort. I fall asleep, and for first time since I came to this place, I dream.

"You're a monster." Maria casts the accusation the moment the locksmith steps through the door. Any illusion of innocence on her part falls away. "I knew it the moment I saw you."

Does she even realize that he is nothing compared to me?

"I saved you." The locksmith frowns, perplexed.

"Like you saved these poor women?" Maria leans forward, so close her breath fogs the glass. "My brothers will find me and, when they do, you will suffer for what you've done."

If I'd had brothers, I wonder if they would have saved me. I wonder if they would have saved my sister.

I doubt it.

"I will make you better," says the locksmith.

"There's nothing wrong with me." Maria turns her back to him, leaving the locksmith to stare at the bridal silk clinging to her shoulders.

The locksmith frowns and strokes his beard with thick fingers. The keys dance under his touch. He hesitates, unsettled. Even though it is Maria's turn, he takes me out instead. I am tender and raw to the touch. I haven't had time to heal, but I ache with anticipation. I need him to finish the rendering. I need a key of my very own, and he is the only one I've found cruel enough to do it.

"Fight him." Maria bangs on the glass separating us.

The locksmith's dead wives provide a gallery for the theater staged on the operating table.

"Let's see about that voice, shall we?"

"Don't let him do this to you." Maria shouts loud enough for both of us.

Doesn't she see? Doesn't she realize this is my only hope?

The locksmith slices me open from chin to sternum, exposing the rot trapped in the flayed layers of tissue and cartilage. He looks for remnants of gills, but they disappeared a long time ago. He turns his attention to my voice box. The locksmith removes the damaged cords and sinew and carefully places them on a metal tray. Out of the corner of my eye, I catch a glimpse of the replacement's golden gears. He installs the clockwork larynx, winds it up, and braids the little golden key in the length of his beard. And in that moment, I realize my remaking is complete.

Maria slumps to the floor of her case. The skin on her knuckles has left little crescents of blood on the walls of her prison. Her face is flushed, her eyes bruised. And her glorious hair has fallen from its confinement to cascade over her shoulders to her waist. She is perched on the precipice of despair, but she shouldn't worry. I know what I am doing. I catch Maria's gaze behind the blood-smeared glass and smile to expose needle-sharp teeth.

The girl's eyes widen, and I know in that moment she has seen me for what I truly am. She scrambles backwards, opening and closing her mouth like a moonfish torn loose from the sea. Slowly, so as not to attract the locksmith's attention, I lift my hand and press a long lean finger against my lips. She clasps both battered hands across her mouth as if attempting to strangle a scream before it can be born.

"Such a lovely specimen," says the locksmith.

I ignore the sound of metal instruments ticking against the tray, as he unfolds the rotting organ where I'd trapped every shout, every scream I'd never uttered. The gears in my clockwork larynx whir and click, as I test the cylinders with a gentle hum.

Perfect.

The locksmith has examined the pieces he's removed from my form, so I'm not surprised when he opens my blighted voice box with surgical precision. The first notes creep out to tempt my bridegroom. The net is cast. I smile.

"What?" The sharp instrument falls from his hand. "What have you *done*?"

For someone who deals in pain, he really should have known better.

A tide of terror and devastation unfurls like smoke from the cursed voice box. I have already lived through that pain. It cannot touch me again. Maria may or may not survive the storm. But the locksmith is doomed. When my voice was still a beautiful thing, it snared men, made them desperate to drown in my arms. Bruised and battered, the song now released from my old voice box twists into a devastation as furious and as deadly as a hurricane. My chosen bridegroom was damned the moment he carried me away from the beach. I had even started to grow fond of his dedicated pursuits. My poor misunderstood monster.

The locksmith falls backwards to the floor in a dead faint. I slip off the operating table and kneel at his side. His eyes roll back behind the lids, leaving only the whites visible. Thick as morning fog, a piercing cry rolls off the metal tray. It descends to rattle the keys in his beard before creeping up his nose. The whites of his eyes turn red with blood.

I cradle his head in my lap as a lifetime of darkness continues to pour out of the damaged voice box. Notes, pointed as daggers, reach for him.

Some of the smaller slights just nip at his flesh, kissing bruises that bloom under the coarse hair on his arms. The larger pains are more dramatic. They peel off skin, break bones, ravage organs. Being unmade is bloody business, but I stay with him until the end.

In a final burst of fury, my unlocked voice shatters all the glass in the room, leaving silence in its wake.

The locksmith's body is too big for me to move, so I leave him where he landed on the floor. His knives are sharp; it doesn't take long to skin his face. When I finish separating the man from his beard, I can finally see his mouth. I kiss him long and deep before I prepare to leave. He would have liked that.

I tie the braids in his beard to one of the discarded, blood-stained ribbons. I know that if I swim deep enough, the bloody beard will turn blue. Perhaps someday I will swim even deeper, to a place where all color fades. With each move I make, the keys rattle, chiming in counterpoint as I exhale through the golden gears. My mouth wraps around the soft sounds as I tongue the syllables.

I turn to address the bloodied brides in their shattered cases and take a deep breath as the words click in place. "My name is Liegia."

Maria watches as I take my leave. I pause in the doorway and untangle the key to her case from our bridegroom's beard.

"Liegia," I say again, a gentle reminder.

The key sings one true note as it lands on the stone floor near her shattered case. Maria doesn't move or speak as I turn away. Each step takes me farther away from the tortured occupants of the bloody chamber. Even though Maria does not follow me, I'm certain that she and I will meet again.

We are kindred spirits. She just doesn't know it yet.

ROTTEN

An apple a day keeps the doctor away.—English Proverb

The fluted bowl shimmers like an oil slick in the dim light of the rainy afternoon. I am not allowed to touch it, but I touch it anyway. I trace the ridges of the design, delighting in the ripples of metallic pink bleeding into an acid green. Purchased in the years before the Great Depression, this piece of carnival glass has retained its place of honor on tables set by the women in my family for generations. It has only one function for my mother. She uses it to display her apples. When it becomes mine, I plan on filling it with polished stones.

Each and every day, my mother eats an apple. During her morning ritual, she sorts through the lot, seeking the one that speaks the loudest. My mother prefers the glossy finish of Red Delicious with their flavorless white flesh and saccharine blandness.

If I had it my way, I would spend more time in the forest, munching on the little green globes growing on the gnarled tree in front of my grandmother's house. I delight in their sour bite and crisp texture. My grandmother presses the crop, bottling it to ferment into hard cider. In the last days of autumn, the remaining fruit falls to the ground in rotting piles. My grandmother says apples are like men. She tells me fresh fruit is boring; it's always better after it has been torn apart and transformed into something else. I wouldn't know.

I'm not allowed to eat my mother's apples. They are hers and hers alone. She polishes them into miniature mirrors reflecting her face. She says those cultivated spheres keep her beautiful. It works too. Men adore her. I watch them watching her. They never see me. I'm too young, too plain to compete with her. She reminds me of this often.

The tempo of the rain increases. The insistent drumming eases my fears of being alone in the quiet darkness. This morning, my mother said she'd be back before lunch, but the clock is ticking down the last hours of the day. I ache in strange places. My stomach rumbles, a plea for nourishment.

One by one, I polish my mother's apples with a mist of breath and a cotton sleeve, but as hard as I try, I cannot find an apple willing to show me my face. They stay silent in their bowl, hoarding their compliments for the woman who loves them more than she loves me. Frustrated and defiant, I pluck the shiniest piece of fruit from the bowl and roll it in my hand, relishing its smoothness and weight before I take a bite.

The sweet rot hits hard. I spit it out and hold the apple up for inspection. A worm has carved a prayer in the pulp. Acid floods my mouth. The apple drops to the floor, and I cover my lips, both hands cupped against the revolt.

If I'd looked closer, would I have seen the hole near the stem? If I'd listened harder, would I have heard their words of warning? *She* would have seen. She would have heard. A fragment of a laugh whispers through the room. I should have known better.

My stomach cramps, tugs down. I run to the bathroom. Bile erupts, a vile stream of yellow staining the toilet and the floor. My gut throbs, and I feel a gush between my legs. I wipe my mouth and look down to see white shorts stained red. A wrenching pain twists low in my stomach. It takes me a moment to realize I'm not a girl anymore.

I'm a woman now.

I kick off my shorts and underwear and shove them in the bathroom trash, covering them with wadded toilet paper. Under the sink, I dig through boxes and try to remember my mother's vague comments on the trials of being a woman. I find a carton of tampons, slender sticks full of cotton plugs. I pull the crisp white covering back, revealing pink plastic prepared to flower. Deep in denial, I toss the stick back in the box and clean up with a wet washcloth before heading back to my room with a roll of toilet paper in hand. Determined to hide my transition, I stuff my underwear full of tissue and get dressed in a pair of black jean shorts. Swaddled in secret, I return to the bathroom to empty the trash and clean the toilet. If I'm careful, she'll never know.

***

Handsome apples are sometimes sour.—German Proverb

"Your daughter looks just like you, Layla," says my mother's newest friend.

I blush at the woman's observation and pretend I didn't hear.

"Don't be ridiculous," says my mother, anger flickering deep in her eyes.

The towel is all I have to cling to, as I scoot into a sun-shaded chair. Chlorinated water drips down my legs and puddles at my feet.

The woman flinches at the barbs in my mother's voice. She backpedals. "I'm going to get another drink. Would you like one?"

My mother shifts on her lounge chair and lifts a hand to wave the woman away. The frowsy blonde's forced smile falters, and she stumbles to her feet. Her skin stretches over plump thighs, and her stomach folds into rippling rolls, as she bends over to shuffle through the bags lumped together on the table. Her body fascinates me. The startling contrast between her pink, lumbering flesh and my mother's firm, tanned form only makes the woman look more awkward.

I can't remember this new friend's name. I gave up trying to keep up with the ever-revolving door of my mother's companions. They never last long.

"One apple martini coming right up," the blonde says, as she holds up her wallet.

My mother closes her eyes under the shaded brim of her sunhat.

The woman's features pinch into a scowl. My mother never frowns. She keeps her face in a smooth emotionless mask, the product of one of her poisonous secrets. Her new friend never learned that lesson. Wrinkles crease the blonde woman's forehead and feather out from the corner of her eyes.

She glances at me. "Do you want anything, Stella?"

I want to tell her that being nice to me will only make my mother madder, but I just shake my head. Layla muzzled me long ago.

The woman sighs and walks away to place her order at the pool bar.

"Stella." My mother's voice is rich and warm. "Come here."

I move slowly, a stone in the pit of my stomach weighing me down. *You stupid little bitch.* The silent words cut more cruelly than the ones she speaks. I want to protest, but I know better. The chair screeches, as I push it back.

"Bring the lotion."

I shuffle over, flip-flops scraping against the rough tiles. She watches me, disdain evident in the tilt of a raised eyebrow. *Lumbering cow.* My towel comes undone, slipping down to expose my bony body loosely covered in a brown bikini. She never wears earth tones. She leaves those to me. Her nail polish matches her red lips, which curve in a smile as sharp as a scimitar.

Her accusations bash around inside my head. *Ugly. Bony. Awkward.*

"You don't look anything at all like me," she says. "If I didn't know better, I would think you belonged to someone else."

I wish it was true.

Her French-cut swimsuit gleams white, accentuating her hourglass figure and bronzed skin. She turns over her palm, and I pass her the suntan lotion. Before she can begin, a man approaches with two drinks in hand.

"You look thirsty." He offers my mother a martini glass filled with a liquid as green as envy. A round, wafer-thin circle of apple floats on the top. I catch a glimpse of the pentagram in the center, a starburst of seeds.

Her eyes narrow as she assesses him. I know he passes her appraisal when she tilts her head and arches her back. Her attention shifts, and she casts her net of seduction, a silvery shimmer spreading out to ensnare a new prey.

"Parched," she says, waving to the empty seat at her side. He grins and sits, placing the drinks on the side table.

Layla's blonde friend stops a few feet away and stares. She holds a drink in each hand. Her face flushes pink, and then she slowly turns to walk back the way she came.

Layla ignores her. "Go play, Stella," she says without looking at me.

I wander over to the sparkling water. A woman frolics in the shallow end with a fearless toddler pushing the limits of his water wings. The rest of the pool is empty, a backdrop for the beautiful people visiting the resort. The cool blue promises a respite from my mother's scathing tongue and hot looks. I raise my hands overhead, preparing to dive. I freeze, peering across the water to her cabana. She looks straight at me and points. Her companion grins and joins the fun.

Heat flushes my face. I'm afraid to look down, afraid of what I will see. I look anyway. The hand-me-down bikini has betrayed me, riding up across my narrow chest to expose budding breasts. *Underdeveloped little runt.* I shrug off her curse and take the plunge. Her words can't reach me here under the waves. If only I could hold my breath, I would stay down here forever.

***

No apple tree is immune from worms.—Russian Proverb

Today, it finally happened. A man watched me with an appraising look most men reserve for my mother. And then he ruined the moment.

"You must be sisters," he said.

Layla laughed, but I could hear the sharp edge in her voice. She pushed me aside and redirected his attention, trapping him with her seductive power in just moments. He didn't look at me again.

I could have despaired, but I figure I've had enough of that in my life. Instead, I went down to the local drug store, lifted a box of hair dye, and went back to the house to orchestrate my transformation while my mother was still away.

Behind the safety of locked doors, I survey the implements arrayed in front of me: one of my mother's new razors, her tweezers, her cherished comb, her sewing kit, and the unboxed color, all neat and tidy in shiny tubes. I shed my clothes and scan my image in the mirror. Unlike my mother's overripe voluptuousness, my body fits on a narrow frame. My breasts are small, but high and firm. My legs are long and lean under the shadow of hair she refuses to let me shave. My heart-shaped face hides behind a chestnut curtain hanging down to my waist.

I start with the most obvious link between us. I pull her comb through my hair, watching the pearled handle glint between my fingers. Some of her magic must be trapped between its teeth because my hair responds, lifting in a nimbus that dances in the air. Only then do I smash the ivory fangs, letting the fragments fall to the floor. Sharp scissors slice through the hated mass, and I revel in the freedom of finally being unveiled. I sweep the heavy locks aside with a bare foot. Short and spiky, my hair makes my face appear sharper, fey. For the first time since I can remember, I smile.

Eager to expand my newfound freedom, I turn on the hot water and sit on the edge of the tub. Foamy lather spurts out of a pink can, and I spread it on my legs, covering the hair in a layer of white. I am cautious, but eager. With each pass, black curdles in white, revealing soft skin. I rinse and repeat. Overly confident, I press too hard on the last stroke. The razor slices. As I watch, blood wells from the cut, falling in three large drops to spread across the white tile. My grandmother's lessons are not wasted. Three wishes tumble past my lips in a breathy rush. Ignoring the stinging cut, I grit my teeth and pick up where I left off. With the last of the foam and hair rinsed off, I step out of the tub and prepare for my final act of defiance.

Steam obscures the mirror. I use a towel to clear a window in the glass, but I have only moments to stare at my own reflection before it clouds back over. My mother speaks to this mirror several times a day. I should have known it was on her side.

Hands encased in plastic gloves, I follow the instructions, mixing color with toner. Guided by touch alone, I apply it to my newly cropped cap of curls. The air pricks at my bare skin and cools my saturated hair. Even though I know I should be ashamed, I revel in the feeling of being comfortable in my own body.

A glance at the clock tells me that my freedom is coming to an end, so I crack the door and listen to the silence of the house before dashing across the hall to my room. Shuffling through the clothes in my closet, I find a plain black sheath given to me by one of my mother's old friends. It will do.

Back in the bathroom, I rinse the dye out of my hair. The color swirls in the sink like a deepening bruise left from one of my mother's barbs. I run one of her immaculate towels across my shaggy curls, and it comes away marked by my rebelliousness. My resolve slips at the sight of the discolored linen, but there is no going back, so I shrug and let it fall to the splotched tiles covered with severed hair.

Disregarding the modesty of underwear, I slip into the chic dress, a gift my mother allowed me to keep only because she thought I'd never be able to wear it. I reach behind and pull up the zipper to where it ends in a deep V at the back. I tug the hem down, but it won't go any farther than mid-thigh. Having second thoughts about my wickedness, I reach for the doorknob but flinch when I hear the front door slam.

My heart pounds, but I push the fear aside. I am someone else. I am no longer her shadow. With the stained towel, I wipe away the last residue of condensation on the glass and peer into the mirror. This time the mirror speaks.

I no longer resemble my mother. A black tumble of short curls frames a pale face. The dress hugs my form, revealing subtle curves from my waist to my hips. The slight mounds of my breasts press against the soft fabric.

"Stella," my mother calls out. "Where are you?"

I stand straight and push my shoulders back, bracing myself for the attack. With a studied grace, gleaned from fifteen years of watching Layla, I walk down the hall. My approach causes her to drop a bag of groceries. *Slut.* Ripe red apples roll across the floor. One stops next to my bare foot, and I lean over to pick it up.

"What have you done?" She chokes on the question. Her mask slips, as a frown pinches her forehead.

I roll the apple in my palm, inspecting it for flaws. It's perfect. "Don't you like it?"

"Stella?" Her mask collapses under the weight of the word. Tiny wrinkles appear on her face. A tear slips down her cheek. "Why did you do this?"

"That's easy." I breathe on the apple and polish it on my dress. When I hold it back up, it reflects my face and tells me that I'm the fairest in the land. I smile and take a bite out of the firm flesh, letting the apple's juice run down my chin. "I got tired of looking like you."

***

When the apple is ripe it will fall.—Irish Proverb

When the weight of winter finally becomes too much for Layla to bear, she drops me off at my grandmother's house in preparation for a vacation in warmer climes. She doesn't want me around to sour her adventures.

"Don't let her out of your sight," she says, not caring that I am standing right next to her. "She's a wicked, spiteful creature."

My grandmother watches my mother with her mild dark gaze until Layla's litany of complaints tapers off.

"You'll see," Layla says, as she stomps out of the cabin. The door bangs shut behind her.

"Good riddance," says my grandmother.

My shoulders relax even though my mother continues a scathing reproach only I can hear. *Ugly bitch.* Even after the car rolls down the long gravel driveway, her words whisper in my ear. *Stupid cow. Cunt.*

My grandmother turns her attention to me and grins. Her teeth are sharp and white behind her blood-red lips. "Now where shall we start?"

I hesitate and stare out the window. Large snowflakes swirl through the air in a thick flurry of white. A frosting of ice silvers the stark black limbs of the trees. Silence spreads in the space between us. Even though the fire crackles and shares its generous heat, a chill skates across my spine.

My grandmother has never resembled the other grandmothers I've met in friends' homes. I know she must be old, but her skin shows only the faintest hints of age. In fact, she doesn't look old enough to be a mother, let alone a grandmother. Her body is long and trim like mine, but she walks with a grace I've yet to learn. Her long hair resembles hammered silver just on the verge of turning liquid. When she moves, the heavy mass floats behind her like a fairy cape. And in the dim illumination of the fire, it appears to be edged with molten red.

"You heart is too tender, my dear." My grandmother opens a cabinet and retrieves a little glass coffin from the shelf. "Let's put it somewhere safe, shall we?"

I find my voice. "Will it hurt?"

My grandmother's smile broadens, and her eyes glitter like black stars. "Only for a moment."

She reaches out to embrace me, one arm wrapped around my waist, the other buried deep in my chest. In the space between one breath and another, my heart flutters in her palm. All the bitterness, the rage, the pain locked away panics in a flurry of fervid emotion. And then it is done.

She releases me and gently places my heart in the glass box. "There now. Isn't that better?"

Everything is the same, but different at the same time. Now that the last of my mother's power over me has been stripped away, I can hear so many things: snowflakes brushing against the frosted windows, the fiery dance of sparks in the hearth, the crush of heavy boots pressing through snow, a human heartbeat moving closer and closer toward the cottage.

The rap of a fist against wood startles me out of a fugue.

"It appears there's a wolf at the door," my grandmother says. "How marvelous."

A strange hunger gnaws at my insides.

My grandmother pats my cheeks. "Wolves love my cider," she says, as she turns my face from side to side in the cradle of her hands, searching. "The beasts are notorious for having a sweet tooth."

"Cider?" The hunger grows, leaving me hollow.

Apparently satisfied, she releases me and steps aside. "Have a good time, my dear." My grandmother plucks her favorite wool cape from its hook. She fastens it around her throat and draws the red hood up to cover her hair. "And try not to make a mess."

She leaves with a stealth born from a life filled with secrets. The latch on the back door snicks shut, but I know the man lingering on the front porch will not be able to hear what I can hear. How could he? Poor thing.

The knock comes again, louder. "Is any one home?"

This time I answer.

***

An apple never falls far from the tree.—English Proverb

The water ripples and rolls, as I shift my weight in the tub. The petrified remains of the wolf's heart rest between my breasts. I have started taking long soaks after that long winter night, but it doesn't matter how many baths I take or how long I stay submersed; there is no washing away the stain of my true nature.

Fragmented memories drift in my mind, as I float in the rose-scented water. I push them aside and concentrate on breathing. Bubbles follow the slopes of my body, rising and falling with each breath. The water starts to chill, and I reluctantly sit up, hand clenched around the bloodstained stone the size of a man's heart. The blackness refuses to give up its hold, no matter how many times I scrub it, but I run my thumb over the stain anyway.

Monster.

I cock my head in the direction of the master bedroom, but the sounds of my mother's dalliance have quieted. Layla and her young lover must be taking a break. Grateful for the reprieve, I slip out of the tub and dry off. The mirror comments on my sleek form, and I smile.

A door shuts, and the hall floor creaks. Steps echo down the hall. Layla has been avoiding me, so I know it's her huntsman who pauses at the door. After a long beat, the footsteps continue in the direction of the kitchen. The grandfather clock in the living room chimes twelve.

I release a breath I hadn't realized I was holding. Earlier in the evening, I heard Layla bragging about stealing her newest lover from a younger woman. She had been inordinately proud of the acquisition of this rugged bounty hunter. Only now, that prize is walking around the house—alone.

Dishes clatter in the kitchen, and I realize I don't have long before he will return to her. In a hurry, I sift through assorted beauty products for rose lotions and powders. Layla once told me roses belong to the apple family. Floral notes sour on her skin, but they complement me perfectly. My grandmother told me so. I finger-comb my damp curls and pinch my cheeks until they bloom. Before I can have second thoughts, I wrap myself in one of Layla's cast-off robes. The shimmering pattern settles around me, revealing dwarfed figures trapped in the weave of scarlet, sapphire, and saffron.

The carpet tickles my feet, as I glide down the hall. I pause in the kitchen. The only piece of clothing on the man's body is a pair of jeans that hang low on his hips. The muscles on his back ripple, as he sorts through the refrigerator. I rock back on my heels and enjoy the view of this huntsman who was brought down by Layla's wiles.

He pulls out a milk carton and shuts the refrigerator door with a bare foot. Even though the kitchen is dim, I can tell the exact moment he sees me. He freezes in place, the milk carton crushed in his grip.

Sensing an advantage, I edge closer and drop the bloodstained stone among the apples cradled in the lurid carnival glass. They scream and wail in despair, but the huntsman is deaf to their warnings.

"Did you find everything you need?"

"I was just making a snack." He shifts his weight and relaxes.

"I'm hungry too." I twist the satin sash holding my robe closed.

He opens his mouth as if he is going to say something, but then appears to think better of it.

"Where's Layla?" I ask, even though I already know the answer.

"Sleeping."

I think of Layla's pill drawer. She isn't the only one with knowledge of poisons.

He watches me with a mixture of fear and lust. I decide to accept both. With a tug on the sash, the robe falls open. I shrug off the silky material and let it pool in a kaleidoscope of color around my feet. An understanding passes between us.

"She said you were heartless." He sets the milk carton the counter.

"Did she?" I smile with the knowledge that my heart is safe in its glass casket, hidden deep in the woods.

"She said you were sleeping."

"I'm awake now." A coy glance reveals the knowledge I desire. He belongs to me now.

This is how I know it's time to move on.

BURNING BRIGHT

There are two identical doors. Behind one is a lady. Behind the other is a tiger.

Which door will you choose? The one on the right, or the one on the left?

Eeny, meeny, miny, mo.

***

A stray gust of wind needled through an eyelet in the tent, which fueled the flame just enough that it was able to reach up to scrape its teeth across her belly, severing the thread that held her skin in place. She fell in a heap of fur and bones to the arena floor. The crowd fell silent for a moment and then roared to life as her trainer snapped the fierce black whip near her face.

"Vega, Vega!" The man's voice was all iron bars and prodding forks. "Up, Vega!"

She shifted to a kneeling position but kept her stomach close to the floor. Her ears flattened against her skull and her lips peeled back in a snarl. The tiger trainer stepped forward and snapped the whip, closer this time. She knew the drill. The trainer might go easy on her if she succumbed now, so she staggered to her feet. Perhaps this was how she'd escape, Vega thought as she waited for her insides to slip through the seams.

Nothing happened.

A flicker of amusement flashed across the tiger tamer's face before his gaze hardened. He forced her through the rest of the routine, an act that revolved around her—Vega, his rising Star.

The crowd cheered.

***

Sometimes a girl is born in a skin that doesn't fit quite right. It might be too loose or too tight. Bias cut missing. A hem sewn too short. When this happens, when a girl is born in an ill-fitting skin, she has a choice. She can force herself to endure what she cannot disguise. Or she can tear it apart at the seams, cut a new shape to fit a pattern of her own choosing.

Sometimes a girl is born in a skin that doesn't fit quite right, but she never gets the chance to make a choice.

Someone else makes it for her.

***

The girl froze in place, but it was too late. A line of red looped around her wrist, a noose pulled tight in a trap she hadn't seen. Her free hand hovered in the air, fingers curled to catch a Star woven from a simple string. The noose tightened.

"You belong to me now," said the boy.

His voice was light whereas his touch was not.

The girl's heart fluttered, but still she didn't move. The green tracery of veins ghosted under sun-warmed skin. With her palm facing down, her pulse remained hidden. For now.

"Say it," he said. "Say you're mine."

That scarlet string pressed harder, so hard that her bones ached.

It had started simply enough. Cradle. Rabbit. Diamond. Crown.

Keeping the line taut, the boy slipped a knot to close the loop. He checked the tension and then added a whole line of knots, one after the other, like beads on a string.

Hunter. Candle. Dragon. Flame.

She searched back through the blur of figures, but she still couldn't see it, that moment when a simple child's game had turned into something else.

The boy brought her hand to his mouth. "Mine," he whispered, the syllable igniting like sulphur sparked to flame. Languidly, he pulled the string between his teeth and severed the loop, leaving the girl at the end of a leash. "You belong to me now."

The boy turned her palm over. He kissed the tender skin with lips firm as the flesh of a plum. The noose slipped beneath her skin and threaded into her veins. The boy measured out a length of red, as the knotted skein followed the radial pathway to the girl's heart. The boy tugged on the string and, once he was certain that it was firmly anchored, he swallowed the other end.

"Say it," he said.

The girl drew in a thin, reedy breath.

The boy raked his teeth along her breastbone. His tongue followed, branding her with trail of leisurely kisses. His eyes were closed. Contentment rumbled deep in his chest.

Tiger. That was the figure he'd camouflaged with clever fingers. No. Not Tiger, but Tyger. A seductive assault. A proclamation of love. Dizzy with the revelation, the girl exhaled and gave him what he wanted.

***

The merry-go-round spins and spins. The mirrors reflect a menagerie of fabulous beasts painted with decorative colors that startle the imagination. How vivid! How bold!

The horses with their jeweled harnesses and cotton-candy colors are accompanied by giraffes, deer, ostriches, dragons, and tigers. Something as beautiful as a hand-carved unicorn must be guarded from vandals, protected from the elements. The poles speared through the creatures keep them steady; the bolts pinning hoof and claw to the floor are an added safety measure.

The lights! The mirrors! A dizzying spectacle of color and charm. The merry-go-round just keeps spinning, one revolution after another. And at the center, the calliope screams.

***

Back in the tight confines of her cage, Vega began to groom herself. Her search for the thread led to the discovery of scarlet stitches that zippered her from tongue to tail. They had not been there before.

The trainer and his newest assistant paused near the beast wagon. The iron bars mocked her own stripes but failed to hide her from prying eyes.

"Is she okay?" The assistant carried buckets filled with the scent of old blood.

"She's young." The trainer tapped a long metal fork against the bars. "It won't happen again."

Even though the threat ruffled her fur, Vega concentrated on unravelling the red thread that held her together.

"Vega will do as I command."

Metal rapped against metal as the trainer sought to capture the tiger's attention. "She belongs to me. She has always belonged to me."

At that, Vega paused with the sudden realization that she'd understood every word, every single one. Hidden beneath the black- and orange-striped fur, the shadow of another life stretched, reaching for freedom. Vega held the thread between sharp teeth and pulled.

***

Even though linings seem like a luxury, any decent dressmaker will tell you that a proper lining is an important step in the sewing process, one that you shouldn't skip. This silky layer is attached to the outer garment and serves many functions: hiding raw edges and internal seams, providing a slippery surface that makes it easier to dress and undress, and keeping areas of tension such as the knees and seat from sagging or stretching.

Although most linings are "invisible," that doesn't mean you shouldn't have some fun with them. Some people choose a lining fabric that matches the garment, but there's no reason you can't select a contrasting color or print instead. Go wild. You'll be glad you did.

***

"I love you," the boy said in between kisses that rained down like blows.

He had found her hiding under the pelt of the tiger he'd killed on safari. Hunched beneath the weight of that orange- and black-striped fur, the girl had spent the afternoon picking at a loose thread she'd found under the bruises that mottled her breasts. She'd pulled and pulled, a pool of red string unraveling in her lap. But no matter how hard she'd yanked on that slender strand, the knots around her heart held.

The boy ripped the pelt from her shoulders and his passion shattered, scoring her in a blaze of white heat. He wrapped his hands around her wrists and forced her to her knees.

"I will never let you go." The boy looped the thread around her, wrapping it tightly around her breasts, her hips, her thighs. "Never."

Under the pressure of his kisses, the bindings sank beneath her skin. The boy caressed the new bruises left behind.

Outside the open window, the stars wept silver streaks against the backdrop of the night sky. The scent of jasmine crept into the room to comfort the girl, but even those sweet notes couldn't mask the mingled odors of sex and blood clinging to her skin.

"You belong to me," the boy said when he finished. "You will always belong to me."

***

Girls go missing all the time.

Some of them return.

Some of them return more than once.

***

During the next performance, the tiger shone brighter than any Star.

"Vega, Vega!" The whip cracked.

The tiger jumped higher, ran faster.

Why do you make me do this? A fist bruised. A spark ignited. The memory burned. A girl held up outstretched fingers, skin tinted orange in the late afternoon light. *Get up*. Another blow fell. The world shattered.

"Up, Vega!"

The tiger roared, setting black stripes rattling against her bony frame. She leaped.

The timing was perfect.

As Vega passed through the blazing ring, she shed the tiger skin and landed right on cue, only this time on two feet instead of four.

Out in the grandstands, beyond the glare of the circus lights, the red wet mouth of anticipation swallowed the audience whole. The trainer's eyes widened. The whip fell from his fingers.

Vega snatched it from the sawdust and easily balanced the heavy handle in her human hand. She grinned, teeth bared, as the whip sliced through the air between them.

The thread snapped.

THE GRAVITY OF GRACE

The first feather sprouted from her scalp on a fine spring morning when Grace, on a dare, defied gravity. She pushed her swing to its highest arc before taking the leap that would prove she was as brave as any boy on the playground—that included Billy, who watched from the swing on her left.

Grace pretended to ignore him, concentrating instead on the feel of the heavy metal links sweating under her grasp. She rocked her feet back and forth, shifting her weight with exaggerated motions. The whole playground spread out around her—the shiny silver equipment, the fresh blue paint, the combed white sand. But behind the bright and cheery exterior, it was just like every other elementary school Grace had ever been to. And she'd been to plenty.

The chains bit into her palms and the cold morning air blew straight up her skirt. As she soared, her long pigtails flared like outstretched wings eager to fly. And then there was a pause before she fell backwards. Her pigtails dropped, coiling around her neck like silky snakes. Feathers and scales. Always feathers and scales, but Grace didn't wear either of them. She hoped she never would. She was just like any other child out there, or so she told herself, even as the boys hooted and hollered, incensed by her dark olive skin only made darker by the modest white skirt rucked up around her bony hips.

Grace was pretty sure all the kids in fourth grade were watching. Maybe the fifth graders too. Her skirt flapped like broken wings as she kicked higher. Let them look. Soon she was so high, she was sure that just one more thrust would propel her straight up and over that metal bar.

"Do it!" Billy shouted as he passed her on the downswing. At the highest point, her arch nemesis took the leap, stocky limbs flailing in the air, arms pinwheeling as he tried to keep upright through the fall. He landed with a wild whoop and looked back at her with a smirk.

"Did you see that?" His golden hair glinted in the early morning light. Billy made a face, taunting her as he stretched his skin at the temples with fingers as pale as the moon. "Or did your mom pull your hair too tight?"

Grace grimaced, but then immediately let her face relax. Any smile, any frown, any expression whatsoever only enhanced the slant of her eyes, a "gift" from her mother. Grace knew she should ignore Billy, keep her momentum in an easy rocking of legs flung forward, bent back. But what was the point of *that?* All the girls did *that.* She had no interest in being one of those bubble-headed girls so popular in the cartoons she was forbidden to watch. She could pretend to have the demure dignity her mother demanded, or she could take the chance to beat the boy at his own game. Grace considered her options as she swung backwards again, pigtails fluttering against her exposed neck.

"I knew she couldn't do it." Billy elbowed his buddy in the ribs. "Little bitch."

Grace knew her father would have been amused at the boy's attempt at cursing, especially since it didn't involve him. He might have even given Billy a few pointers. Martin Estrella was a million times meaner than any living person. She didn't need the police to verify the fact with their papers and promises. Her father had written his own commandments on the skins of his daughters. She had the scars to prove it.

But Martin Estrella had disappeared the day her sister died. He'd sacrificed Ava in the hopes that his daughter's blood would seal his desire to become a living god. When it didn't work, he'd fled, and Grace hadn't seen him since. Martin couldn't hurt her. Not anymore. She gritted her teeth and jumped.

Grace curled her fingers into claws. She leaned forward, stretching out her slim ten-year-old frame in an effort to reach the bully and his friends. She would crush them, all of them, destroy them where they stood. In her sudden rage, she could almost taste their blood in her mouth. But she couldn't fly; all she could do was fall.

In that one frantic moment, Grace attempted to reconnect with the swing. Her arms pinwheeled. Her legs kicked. And then, she crashed to earth, just inches from Billy's feet.

"Holy shit!" Billy stared.

"Run," said the lanky kid next to him. "We gotta get outta here."

The soles of scuffed tennis shoes, skinny jean-clad legs, and a cloud of dust were the only evidence of the boys' retreat. The other kids, who'd gathered to poke fun at the new girl, retreated as well, but Grace hardly noticed. She was too busy trying to catch her breath.

After what seemed like forever, Grace rolled to her side with a groan and forced herself upright into a sitting position. Blood rolled down her knees in thin branching streams, staining the neat white folds of her socks. Sand stuck to exposed skin. Torn lace drooped from her skirt's hem.

"No, no, no." Grace tried to press the lace back together, desperate to hide the evidence of her fall. Smeared red stains competed with the dirt smudged on her wrinkled skirt. Grace let go. Her fingers flitted nervously to her sides, and she sat there for a few moments, almost wishing her father was still around so she wouldn't have to face her mother's disappointment. Back when they'd been a family neither Grace nor Ava existed as far as their mother was concerned, and right now that would have been just fine.

The first bell rang, but Grace ignored it. Resolutely, she assessed the damage and began to pick the coarser bits of gravel out of her scraped palms. She was interrupted in her ministrations by a sharp pain lancing her scalp. *Stupid pigtails,* she thought, wishing she could gnash her teeth. It sounded so ferocious, like something Martin would do. But she was only a girl, not some wild thing, or so her mother said.

Grace reached up and tugged on the elastic bands confining her hair. Defiantly, she pulled them out, one by one, and braced herself for the discomfort that always came when she let her hair down. The tingling sensation was so intense it almost burned, but this time it felt different. Not like a concussion though; not like the times Martin had left her so rattled she'd been unable to stand for hours. She might have been bruised and bleeding, but her thoughts stayed clear. No double vision. No dizziness. No nausea.

Grace ran her fingers through the thick black curls, hoping to shake the odd sensation, but stopped when the silky fan of a feather brushed her fingertips. Grace froze with the feather resting between her thumb and forefinger. She tugged, but it stayed put. She tugged harder and winced, trying not to think about the last time her hair had been pulled. Even so, she could almost feel Martin's fist curled around her scalp as though it was an egg he could easily crush. Grace braced herself, then yanked the feather good and hard, right where the shaft protruded from the skin.

The slender plume lay cradled in the cup of her skinned palm. She marveled at the deep crimson color. A voice of reason, her mother's, urged her to throw it away, but she couldn't bear the thought of anyone else picking it up. It was *hers*, not something shed by a dirty bird. It made her think of the fearsome mask favored by her father, but even that wasn't enough to dissuade her. This feather was as red as the blood smeared across her abraded knees, not the iridescent black crowning Martin Estrella's wicked winged mask on display in her mother's living room.

Grace curled her fingers around it.

Memories of Martin whispering to her in the dark urged her to hide the feather, proof of her monstrous heritage. Her mother would take it away, destroy it. Purification by fire. Grace tucked it in the bodice of her stupidly old-fashioned dress and stood up. The slender red feather belonged to her, and she wasn't going to let anyone take it away—not ever.

***

Grace was sent home early. Her mother Feng waited at the door. She took one long look at the devastation. There was no maternal mercy in those amber eyes; they saw everything. It took all of Grace's resolve to not fidget. Feng turned her back and started down the hall.

Grace bowed her head and followed. As she passed the sleek table pressed up against the foyer wall, Grace slipped the feather out of her bodice and deposited it in one of the vases crowding the surface. She chose the container she hated the most to shield her prize. The slender white one, etched with a pastoral scene from her mother's homeland. The phoenix hovering on the imaginary horizon only sharpened the dig, a reminder that Grace could never have her mother's power over fire. However, the vase was the one place Feng wouldn't look. No one dared to touch the sacred things on her mother's altar, not even Martin Estrella.

Once in the bathroom, Feng finally addressed her. "Take it all off." Each word rolled from her tongue like a mini heatwave. Grace could trace the path of golden fire pulsing in the hollows of Feng's throat. Had Grace been born with her mother's gift, she was sure she'd have been burned alive. Feng kept her emotions tightly controlled: one of her mother's many feminine traits Grace had failed to master.

Grace looked away and slithered out of the ruined dress. She submitted to her mother's examination under the bright lights. The reflection in the mirror appeared to show a much younger girl, a girl with shadows cutting like bars under each rib. Pink and white scars curved along her collarbones and shoulders, others criss-crossed her narrow hips and tapered to her belly button before disappearing beneath the white cotton underwear.

"What have you done?" Her mother grabbed a handful of hair and pulled Grace's head back. Grace knew better than to look her mother in the eye. She did it anyway.

"You are a wicked child," said Feng.

She let go of her, picked up a brush. The polished handle gleamed like a moonbeam in her mother's golden hand. The thick black bristles quivered as if eager to taste Grace's pain.

"Your sister never would have been goaded into acting like a savage," said Feng.

Nope. But look at which one of us is still alive.

"How many times have I told you to stay away from boys?" She pulled the brush along Grace's scalp so hard it yanked her head back with each stroke. "And now look at you, all bloody and *ruined* and there's nothing I can do to hide it."

Grace kept her lips pressed tight against her teeth. *Seen, but not heard*, she reminded herself.

"Don't you want to be pretty when your daddy comes home?"

No.

But Grace still didn't say anything, even though she hadn't seen her daddy in close to a year. The brush handle slapped the bathroom counter. Grace flinched.

"Do you know what he'd do if he found out you were playing with *boys*?"

Feng switched to a comb with sharp silver teeth that raked Grace's scalp, but she knew better than to protest.

"They're vicious little beasts," she continued.

Grace stared at the unruly curls set free. No matter how long or how hard it was brushed, the locks refused to be smoothed. In sharp contrast, the fall of her mother's hair looked like a bolt of black silk.

"Stay away from them, *all* of them." Grace's mother took the left half, the side where she'd sprouted the red feather, and yanked it into a high pigtail, pulling the strands tighter with each brushstroke until it was just smooth enough to tie in place. "Don't make me tell you again."

The spot where Grace had plucked the feather was still tender, but her mother didn't seem to notice the wound, and Grace wasn't about to draw attention to it. Feng switched sides.

"We have to look nice when he gets back." Her mother's voice trembled, just the tiniest bit, but her golden composure held. "Your daddy likes his girls pretty."

Tears glittered, but they didn't fall. Grace had her mother's eyes, but the lower half of her face resembled that of her father. Her nose was too broad, her lips too full. She hated her father for bestowing her with his blood-soaked heritage, the feathered serpent's lies that had seduced her mother into believing Martin Estrella was her true match. Even though his claims were rooted a world away from Feng's homeland, his dragon had succeeded in seducing the firebird, the only one of her kind. He'd sought power from this union of yin and yang, but it hadn't been enough. The blood sacrifices hadn't been enough either. Her mother still had hope he'd transform into a god worthy of her love. Hope was all she left.

"I'm sorry," Grace whispered.

A band snapped high on her head, securing the other pigtail in place.

"I know you are." Her mother's calm cracked a little more. Fiery points of light swam close to the edges of her skin, seeking a way to consume them both.

Grace grabbed at words that sprouted from her lips as surely as the feather had rooted in her hair. Memories of Martin calming her mother surfaced. He had found incantations that controlled the firebird lurking beneath Feng's skin. Grace mimicked the words. She swallowed the strange language and held it against the roof of her mouth in the way she'd seen her father do. The incantation growled in the back of her throat. Even though Feng didn't appear to hear the spell, her brightness dimmed, and then vanished altogether.

"I need to go lie down," she said. "Be a good girl and clean this mess up."

Her mother stepped over the stained dress and left Grace alone. The bathroom was suddenly cold. Grace stared into the mirror, hoping to see a difference in her appearance. Her scalp throbbed in a dull steady reminder of the feather, a pain similar to the aches on her skinned knees and palms, but deeper. Her dark hair had been pulled so tight her face felt as though it would split down the middle. The result left her looking more alien than ever. Not for the first time, she wished she'd been born to normal parents, people without a legion of secrets hidden behind every move they made.

Grace searched the glass for her father's face, but the reflection stayed flat.

"I hope you are dead, you lousy snake," she said.

In her heart, she knew her father was still on the run somewhere, but if he did show back up, she didn't want to be pretty. Pretty hadn't helped her mother any, and it had gotten her sister Ava killed.

Defiant, Grace went into the living room and stole her mother's prized embroidery scissors out of the sewing basket. The gold-tinted metal swooped in the shape of a bird crafted from flames. Back in the bathroom, she snipped at her pigtails with the sharp blades of the bird's stylized beak until nothing was left but nubs of hair bound by elastic. She cut that too, freeing a short halo of hair that seemed to float around her face. Grace smiled at her reflection. The Grace in the mirror looked cunning and cruel. The girl in the mirror looked like her father, a man who would do anything to claim his heritage as a god. Grace's smile flattened. She flinched at the sting of a feather pushing its way through her hair. She slapped at it, but then another emerged near her hairline. The stings zipped from one side of her head to the other in a flurry of scarlet feathers suddenly sprouting from her scalp, as if the shorn field of her skull demanded replacements.

No, no, no.

As quickly as they emerged, Grace plucked them. Soon the sink was littered with red plumes lining a nest of chopped black curls. When the last of them had been pulled, she carried them to her room. There she laid them out side by side on her bedspread and went to retrieve the single feather she'd brought home from school. In that moment, she decided that no matter what, someday she'd find a way to fly away, fly so high nothing would ever bring her back down to earth.

***

Years passed. In another house in another city, Grace pushed the door open. Inside it looked the same as their houses always did, no matter how often they moved. Feng's home was her nest, and she did everything within her power to fill it with light and memories of her homeland.

It always took a few moments to adjust. Not only was every single curtain pulled back to greet the day but, even on the sunniest afternoons, the light from dozens of silk-draped lamps added another level of brilliance to the room. The furniture, modern and sleek, crouched low to the ground. The yellow seats were deep and scattered with pillows the color of a roaring fire. The long table pushed against the wall gleamed under the burden of Feng's vases, some of which were filled with waxy resins simmering with the scents of sandalwood and sulphur.

Feng had her rules. And Grace delighted in breaking them, especially the one about boys. What did her mother really know anyway? Jason had been the first to befriend her when she'd been forced to switch schools—again. Not only was he kind, but he was fun to be around. His smile seemed brighter than fire, so she'd invited him over to hang out while Feng worked at the hospital. Her mother would never know. Grace grinned at the thought.

"Whoa," Jason said.

"Yeah, it's over the top." Feng wouldn't be home for hours. They could make popcorn and watch a movie or two. Maybe he'd even kiss her.

"Come on." Grace tugged at his suddenly limp hand, but he ignored her.

She followed his gaze to the dragon mask dominating the corner. As always, it was draped in shadow. He shouldn't be able to perceive it. Jason was just a boy. He didn't come from a family imbued with old magic. She backpedaled. All thoughts of popcorn and movies and kisses disappeared. Grace looked around the room as if seeing it for the first time. Bringing a boy home had been a mistake.

"Umm, I changed my mind." She tried to redirect his attention. "Let's go to the mall instead."

Jason shook off her grip and stepped onto the rug.

"Hey," Grace yelled. "You have to take your shoes off."

But it was too late; patches of brown smudged the pristine pile. Grace pinched the bridge of her nose.

"Totally dope." He skirted the couches and headed straight for the mask.

There was only one reason a mortal would be able to see the evil thing through the shadows surrounding it, and that reason was unthinkable. The whispers issued from the mask grew bolder, almost loud enough for the sounds to form words. Grace stumbled to a stop. The last time she's heard the mask speak had been the day her sister had died.

"Daddy?" she whispered.

Jason reached up.

"Don't touch it!" Grace yelled, leaping, nearly flying.

Jason's shoulders dropped a fraction. He glanced at her. That extra moment was just enough. Grace threw herself against him. Jason caught her as though she weighed nothing at all.

"Hey, babe." Frown lines pressed between his brows, but his lips parted in a cheeky smile.

The mask recited the names of the girls Martin had sacrificed in his attempts to attain godhood. "Brittany, Tara, Rebecca, Sara, Danielle, Ava."

Grace flinched. Her sister Ava had been dead and buried for five years.

Other names issued forth from the dark-winged mask, names Grace had never heard before. "Angelica, Lucero, Tamara...."

"I like you too, Grace." Jason set her down warily. "But I don't want to rush into anything."

Grace held a fist to her mouth, attention fixed on the fearsome mask.

"Hey." The boy rested a hand on her shoulder. "Are you okay?"

The names looped back to the beginning. And then she saw it. Her father's wind jewel, the conch shell necklace she'd never seen him without, peeked out from the screen of obsidian feathers. It was swinging as if just placed there.

"You have to leave." Her voice choked on memories of her father's little knives kissing her collarbones.

"Grace? What's wrong?"

But it was too late.

"Hey, baby girl." Martin Estrella left the shadows of the hallway and crossed the living room. His steel-toed boots crushed the pile of Feng's white rug. "Introduce me to your friend."

Her mother's warnings echoed in her head. *Do you know what he'd do if he found out you were playing with* boys?

"Daddy?" Grace's teeth chattered.

It had been five years since she'd last seen him. Five years since her sister had died. Five years of safety. Of course, it couldn't last. She was a wicked child, and there was a price to be paid, a blood price.

Jason stepped away from her and stood a little straighter as he faced her father. "Sir," he said, arm extended, palm open for a handshake.

"None of that." Martin Estrella smiled, sending shivers down Grace's spine. "We're all family here." He ignored the boy's hand and pulled him into a bear hug. "Call me Martin," he said, patting Jason on the back like they were long-lost friends.

"Yes, sir." Jason stiffened and pulled away. Red spots bloomed on his cheeks. "Um, Mr. Martin."

But her father kept his arm wrapped around Jason's shoulder. "Grace has never brought a boy home before." His black eyes glittered with amusement. "Have you, baby?'

"No, Daddy."

He looked just like he had the last time she'd seen him. Her father was as trim and fit as ever, his muscled form on display in a white T-shirt with its sleeves rolled up. Grace stared at the feathered serpent tattooed on her father's bicep. The blacks and greens rippled as he flexed.

"We were just hanging out, sir."

"Hanging out, huh?" Martin slapped his free hand against Jason's chest, but his tone was as good-natured as ever. "I've been known to hang out with a pretty girl myself. A guy's gotta have a good time every now and then, right?"

"Yes, uh, no." Jason struggled in Martin's grip.

"But you should know better than to hang out without a chaperon at your age." Martin's smile was so wide it looked like he could swallow the boy whole. "You wouldn't want to ruin a girl now, would you?"

Martin let Jason go. The boy stepped backwards, putting some space between them.

"Sorry, sir." His gaze darted from Grace to her father. "It won't happen again."

"You're right, son."

Martin took the mask off the wall and slipped it over his head. He turned, knives glittering in each fist, and attacked the boy. Grace opened her mouth to scream, but no sound came out. She slid down the wall in a crumpled heap, unable to look away. Jason would never kiss her. He'd never whisper sweet nothings in her ear. He didn't even have time to call for help. Her father made sure of that. When Martin was finished with the boy, Feng's white rug was drenched in blood.

Martin wiped the knife blades on his jeans and flipped them shut with the flick of his wrists before tucking them back in his pockets.

"Well, look at my little girl." He squatted in front of her and smiled through the mask. "You're all grown up."

He picked up the wind jewel from where it lay next to her on the floor and fastened the chain back in place. Grace peeked up at her father. Bright red streaks stained his white shirt. Spatters of blood decorated his arms and hands. Grace gingerly reached out to touch his shoulder.

"Daddy?"

"Don't worry, baby." He covered her hand with his own. "That boy won't be bothering you anymore."

The scales on the mask shifted. The whispers had been replaced. Now it was her father's lips that moved in the hole where the mouth had been.

"I've missed you," he said.

Her scars burned under Martin's fingers. The mask's feathers brushed her cheek, and for the first time, she wished she'd kept her own feathers instead of pulling them out. Perhaps they would have protected her. But there was no stinging distraction, no promise of pinions pushing through her hair. All evidence of her defiance lay trapped in a shoebox under her bed.

Even though the mask was mute, the litany of names circled round and round in her head. How many girls had her father sacrificed in his quest for godhood? Had they suffered like Ava? She thought of all the times over the last five years when the mask had been missing and then found again. Feng had never said a word about those disappearances. Feng never talked about Ava, either.

"Why don't you go change while I clean this up?" The mask's feathers tickled her cheek as her father bent close. "You want to look pretty for me, don't you?"

She nodded and closed her eyes.

"Yes, Daddy."

Her mother *would* be proud.

***

Although Grace had been in college and living on her own for nearly a decade, she still felt like a child whenever she was summoned to her mother's house. The doorbell's chime reverberated through her bones as though they belonged to a bird instead of the girl she used to be. Part of her hoped Feng wouldn't answer, even though that desire was unfounded. Grace was required to attend her mother's fancies when it came to *special* dates. And today was extra special, as far as Feng was concerned.

Sometimes Grace wondered how she'd survived this long. Not only had she finished high school mostly intact, but she'd escaped her mother's clutches when she'd left for college. Grace had tried to walk away from her supernatural legacy, but her father eventually tracked her down. Martin believed himself a god. He insisted the laws of mortals had not applied to him, that his search for transformation called for the blood of innocents. She'd proved him wrong. During their last encounter, Martin had been the one to bleed.

She pressed the doorbell again. While she waited, Grace tugged on one of the wispy filoplumes hidden in her hair. The promise of that pulling sensation helped ease her anxiety, so much so she'd been able to leave the stiff red feathers alone for the first time in more than a decade. Now that they'd grown out, there were more than a dozen of them scattered through her hair. It had even started a fad among the co-eds. Theirs were tied in with ribbons or thread, of course, but they all thought hers were too. Silly geese.

Feng opened the door. She looked Grace up and down, a slow examination that left Grace fidgeting as though she was a child waiting to be judged and punished.

"You've been busy, I see." Feng's scathing appraisal settled on the red feathers peeking out from Grace's unruly black curls.

"Mother."

Feng shifted her attention to the battered shoe box held in Grace's white-knuckled grasp. "What's this?"

"May I come in?" Grace hugged the box to her chest. "I have something to show you."

Feng remained still and silent for a moment, her irritation evident in the grim golden swirl of light coursing just under the skin of her bared arms. She wore a formal qipao, the white full-length silk gown embroidered with her namesake. The phoenix bristled with fiery energy; its sharply defined feathers spread across the backdrop in spiced shades of saffron, cinnamon, fennel, and clove. More ceremonial than functional, the dress only came out of its protective casing once a year.

"Very well." Feng stepped aside, allowing just enough space for Grace to slip past.

Even with sunglasses firmly in place, the brightness inside made her wince. As she adjusted to the intense light, Grace noticed the front room still matched her memories. Feng might have moved a half a dozen times in the years Grace had been away at college, but the placement of her possessions remained the same as though Feng believed she could reshape foundations and walls at will. And perhaps she could. Feng guarded her secrets, for all the good it did her.

Grace noted the presence of Martin's black-plumed mask hanging on the wall and smiled. She slid into a low-slung side chair and balanced the box, lid tightly shut, on her lap. Feng closed the door with a firm hand but lingered in the foyer. The click of a lighter and the scent of sulphur betrayed her mother's unease. Grace nearly laughed at the thought of Feng being anything but calm and composed.

"I always wondered if you'd just picked August 25 for the hell of it, or if you'd actually been born human." Grace picked at the corner of the shoebox lid. "How old are you, anyway?"

"Don't be absurd." Feng's heels clicked on the wood floor, as she crossed the room. She chose a place on the loveseat opposite to where Grace sat. Her elegance and beauty added another layer of warmth to the room. She held her back ramrod straight, ankles crossed, as she struck a formidable pose. Power rippled off her bare arms like the heat trapped in a mirage. Grace could almost see the promise of flaming wings take shape. No wonder Martin Estrella felt he'd finally found his match.

"You could have at least made an attempt to look civilized." She waved a dismissive hand. "Really, Grace. What will your father think?"

Despite her resolve, Grace shifted in her seat. She reached up to tug on a feather, producing just enough pain to help steady her nerves. "How much do you know about who he was? *What* he was?"

The amber color of her mother's eyes took on a reddish hue, the only visible cue of her agitation.

"I think you know more than you let on," Grace said, moving the box from her lap to the glass table standing between them. She tapped the cardboard lid and grinned. "Aren't you even a little curious?"

Feng raised a finely arched brow.

"You were supposed to be better than this." Her gaze pointedly lingered on the deep V of Grace's unbuttoned shirt front. "You were supposed to be *special.*"

"Like Ava?"

"You don't know what you're talking about," Feng said, dismissing the girl's death with the flick of her wrist. "It was a mistake. A tragic accident."

"No, it wasn't." Grace leaned forward, propped her elbows on her knees. "I was there."

Feng pressed her lips together in a tight line. For the first time, Grace saw her mother as a human woman. Lines feathered out from the corners of her eyes and her skin carried an undertone the color of ash. No woman could live forever, not even one as powerful as Feng.

"I also know why Ava's blood didn't release the feathered serpent."

Feng paled but didn't confirm or deny Grace's suspicion that Ava had only been a half-sister. In the end, Ava had been like all the other girls Martin Estrella had sacrificed at the demands of a god. There was no power in the blood of innocents. No power coursing through the veins of mere humans.

Grace pushed the box the rest of the way across the table. "Open it."

Feng looked at the mask hanging silent on the wall and then to the front door where scented smoke lingered.

"He's not coming," Grace said. "Open the box, Mother."

Heat rolled off Feng's bare arms. Golden fire illuminated her skin from the inside out. The delicate white silk withered under the heat. In a smooth motion, Feng flicked the lid off the box with manicured nails shellacked a red as deep and vibrant as the plumes embroidered on her dress. She craned her neck and hissed at the contents. The feathers inside lifted on the exhalation. A few spilled out of the crammed container to rest on the glass separating mother from daughter.

"How dare you bring those vile things into this house?" Feng reached for her daughter's manifest sins. The feathers erupted in flame under her touch. She stood up and turned her attention to Grace.

"I finally figured it out," Grace said. "I'm the real dragon, not him. The feathers prove it."

"You are a wicked, spiteful girl." Feng stepped around the table, blazing arms stretched out in front of her. "I should have done this a long time ago."

But Grace had learned a few lessons from Martin. She pulled a knife from its hiding place in her boot and swiped the sharp blade up between those fiery hands. The steel sliced her mother's throat. Blood spilled, staining white silk red.

Feng ignored the fatal wound. Instead of attempting to stem the tide, she lunged forward and pulled Grace to her in a tight embrace even as she fell to the floor. Flames danced along the forms of both mother and daughter even though only one of them protested. By the time Grace was able to disentangle herself from her mother's self-immolation, her clothes had turned to ash. The scent of burning feathers filled the air.

Grace crawled away from the flames towards Martin's mask. Every inch of her body had been touched by her mother's unearthly fire, yet still she inched towards the only magic left within reach. She'd killed both Martin and Feng, and as such had expected the mantle of godhood bestowed in exchange for the sacrifice. But she was as wrong in her beliefs as Martin had been. Her blood had not been pure, after all. And she'd been so sure. Tears of pain and frustration seared her cheeks.

Scents she associated with her mother—sandalwood, cinnamon, sulphur—hung thick and heavy in the smoke filling the room. Grace's body protested and she collapsed just inches from the wall where the winged mask hung. A curling, howling hunger raced through her veins. Through the smoke, she detected the dusty hint of feathers and scales. But it couldn't be. She'd skinned the monster and buried him herself.

"Daddy?" Her voice was dark with blood and ash.

The mask fell to the floor in a heap of black feathers. Grace reached for it, but stopped, her hand hovering just above the feathered serpent's mask. She gasped as her skin stretched and then split. The burned sections sloughed off in strips. Underneath, gold and amber scales glimmered in the light cast by the blaze of Feng's funeral pyre. Grace sat up, frantically peeling at the raw and blistered skin on her chest and abdomen to reveal the serpent's skin beneath. The scales rippled in an intricate pattern along her ribcage, but a few patches of her humanity remained, unscarred expanses spread out across the softer curves of her belly, breasts, and thighs. The familiar sting zipped across her scalp, but the emerging plumes didn't stop there. Long, stiff flight feathers pierced down the length of each arm. A soft crimson down sprouted along the winged spread of her collarbones, across her navel, dipping down to coat the space between her thighs—the final stages of her apotheosis.

Grace picked up the mask. The black feathers glistened as though they were coated with oil. Darkness dripped from her fingers. Holding it between thumb and forefinger, she carried the hateful thing to the growing blaze and flung it into the fire. The mask's whispers turned to shouts as it burned. The heat intensified. Within the screen of rising flames, a loud crack shattered the screams. Out of the flames, dozens of birds took flight. An ascension of swallows rose first. They swirled around the room, battering themselves against the large picture window.

Grace raised her hands to shield her face and rushed to unlock the front door. Other birds rose from the flames: a raft of mandarin ducks with their distinctive eye stripes and flared crests; a pandemonium of parrots screeching insults in shades of red, yellow, and green; and a violent pride of peacocks scattering embers from their elaborate tails. A few of the birds escaped out the open doorway, but many more remained trapped in the burning room. Desperate, Grace grabbed her mother's prized white vase from its place on the altar and hurled it at the picture window. Glass shattered, but Grace didn't stop. She couldn't stop. Other relics followed, breaking away the jagged edges from the frame until the entire space had been cleared.

The mad confusion of wings veered towards the open space. The swallows, ducks, parrots, and peacocks soared out the window to the bright bowl of sky outside. A few long-legged cranes followed the madness in a flurry of black and white, their red jeweled crowns lighting the way.

Grace moved closer to the door and took one last look at the pyre. Coals skittered out from the conflagration as a large golden pheasant rose from the flames. In her talons, the bird grasped a coiled snake painted in a mottled pattern of malachite and obsidian. In all her golden glory, the pheasant spread her fiery feathers and cast a baleful eye at Grace. For a moment it seemed as though the creature would attack, but then the serpent shifted, and the bird's attention redirected to her prize and the promise of escape. Feng's wings whipped the embers in a glittering cloud, as she rose from the fire and soared out the window in a blaze of light.

Grace stepped outside and watched the birds fly into the sun. She wondered if Feng remembered her human life or if she'd finally cast it off forever.

Feathers and scales. Feng would be proud. Reveling in her transformation, Grace lifted her arms. They *both* would be proud.

MORE WINGS THAN THE WIND KNOWS

There are more wings than the wind knows
Or eyes that see the sun
In the light of the lost window
And the wind of the doors undone.
~Excerpted from "The Ballad of St. Barbara" by G. K. Chesterton

Ancient stories describe the fates of unfortunate souls who have suffered from the terrible curse of beauty. Men loved by the gods turn to flowers—the short-lived anemone, the white narcissus, the tear-stained hyacinth. But those of the fairer sex rarely survive such attacks. Instead, their youth is stripped like leaves from a bough, their bones hollowed into flutes, their faces smoothed into paper masks.

Those are the lucky ones.

***

Alone in the temple, I tend my duties while singing songs learned in childhood. As though summoned by the mournful lament, the sea king rises from the surf in a clash of waves upon the water. There is no place to flee, no hero to save me. The notes shatter under the swiftness of his storm. He conquers the fear my beauty provokes by breaking me into pieces. He severs my promises in one swift stroke and binds my invisible wings in a golden net cast through sinew and bone before leaving me bloody and torn, crowned by an olive branch—a sacrifice on the altar to pay penance for the crime.

She will never forgive me.

A cry catches in my bruised throat. The pressure behind it builds, forcing the sound to escape through cracked lips in a tortured hiss. The world is too bright, too sharp too bear. Beneath me, the cool marble scrapes flesh exposed by the tattered remains of my tunic.

His spent desire collects in tidal pools trapped in the salt-stained hollows of my throat, belly, and hips. I want to run away, but my limbs are pinned by a trident's jagged tips, my locks a tangled chain anchored to stone columns. I want to scream and rage, but my voice is muffled, smothered under the accusations roared in the surf breaking against the white cliffs.

The virgin goddess of wisdom finds me like this, a beautiful broken thing staked to her pristine altar in a parody of supine worship.

"I heard you seducing him, calling to the sea with your siren's song." A star shines on her forehead, a mark of her divine right, as she judges me.

Did you hear my screams?

"I've been watching you." Each word hammers a shard of guilt into my chest. "I've seen the way you walk, the way you tempt with your careless smiles."

Where were you?

"And then you defile my temple with your unholy lust." Her grey gaze pierces me.

It's not true. Make it not true. "Give me courage." My tongue, tattered and torn, struggles to form the words, a mantra to her attributes. "Give me strength." I force the plea past bloody teeth. "Give me justice." *Save me.*

I am doomed.

"I will grant you the justice you deserve."

My hair, my greatest vanity, has remained loose and uncut since that day so long ago when the fatherless boy I once loved spent an afternoon combing the thick, glorious mass while he sang old hymns.

As soon as she says the words, my tangled tresses transform. They curl and coil in a writhing mass around my head. Silk turns to scales that brush against the nape of my neck. Screams harden into stones that settle in the pit of my stomach.

"Leave now," says the virgin goddess of truth and justice. "And never return."

A yellow-striped viper with a scarlet crown kisses my bruised lips with the flicker of a forked tongue. The other serpents crowd close to my skull, bound to me as I am bound to them. *Hurry,* they whisper. *Flee this place. Run while you can.*

I push away from the cold, white altar and stumble to my feet. Through the halls of salvation I run, leaving a bloody trail behind as a testament to innocence lost. There is no one to catch me, as I fall down the steps. My wings flutter in a feeble attempt to restore balance in a world turned upside down, but fear binds them tight, and I land on my hands and knees, head bent under the unfamiliar weight of my hissing locks.

A man stops and stares as I pull myself to my feet. Caught in the snare of my gaze, he freezes in place as his body slowly turns to stone. Despair turns to vengeance. Fury boils in the pit of my stomach. There are others too, countless men left along the trail, as I retreat to the sanctuary found the caves from my youth.

By the time I arrive in my homeland, I am past the fear of the sea and its king. He can't hurt me anymore than he already has. But I cannot harm him either. Such is the fate of a mortal woman.

Unable to avenge myself, I turn my deadly beauty loose on the men bent on conquering a monster. Statues abound in the wild garden crowning the cliffs riddled with the caves where I sleep. Their lust and fear stoke the rage simmering in the pit of my stomach.

I spend hours each day polishing their petrified remains.

At night, my serpents stretch to caress bare flesh. They coil around my thighs and waist. They stroke my arms and shoulders. They tickle my neck and whisper in my ears. *Burn them,* they hiss. *Destroy them all.* Absently, I stroke the red crown of the yellow-striped viper even as my caged wings flutter against the golden net pinning them against my spine.

One morning, I wake to find a hero making his way through my garden. He pays no mind to the tormented statues he passes. Nor is he tempted by the glorious fruit hanging from the trees. My serpents urge me to destroy him, but I ignore them and follow the stranger as he makes his way down the cliff to the labyrinth I call home.

He pauses at the cave mouth in front of two twisted piles of blackened stone—gorgon sisters created from rage spewed forth in a flood of fiery lava and volcanic ash. I test the air, eager to catch the smell of fear. Instead, I am greeted with the sweet scent of anticipation, as the stranger traces the twisted shapes with his sun-bronzed fingers. I can almost feel the hands of the boy I once loved smoothing my hair's luxurious waves.

The serpents coil and writhe around my face, breaking the illusion. *Kill him*, says the striped serpent. *Kill him now.*

I ignore the venomous demands and hissed warnings and follow the hero as he creeps through the tunnels. The torches flicker as he passes. In one hand he carries a sword and in the other a polished shield. This hero is no match for me. I know it, but I wait and watch anyway. There is something familiar in the length of his stride and the way his dark hair curls at the nape.

The man stops at the underground spring flowing at the heart of the maze. He stares at the altar I have carved into the limestone walls. A pile of obsidian tears glitter in the diffuse rays of sun streaming through a narrow skylight overhead. Flowers and fruit rest near trophies taken from my victims. But above it all hangs a leather thong tooled with the impression of tiny roses. A harp carved from rosewood dangles from the thin strap—a gift from the boy I loved, the fatherless boy who once serenaded a girl already pledged to the whims of a goddess and her temple by the sea. The man drops his sword and shield.

"No." A strangled cry escapes his lips. "It can't be."

Oh, but it is.

At the sound of his voice, a thousand little memories of my human life crash down upon me. The fires churning in my stomach dim.

"Em?" He spins around, and I close my eyes even though I want nothing more than to gaze upon the face of the boy I loved so long ago.

A moment of silence stretches between us, and then I hear the shuffle of his sandals scraping against the cave floor. The snakes snap and hiss, but he ignores their warnings and presses his lips against mine. I relax into his embrace for a moment but then push him away. The serpents writhe around my head in an agitated dance.

"Why have you come here?" I already know the answer, but I'm not ready to destroy the destroyer.

"It doesn't matter anymore." His despair flattens the words. "What have they done to you?"

If I open my eyes, I can keep him here with me—forever. But he is the one man in the world I can never hate. In that instant, the last of my rage cools. The goddess, my accuser, made me a monster but not immortal. At least I have that. And if I am doomed to leave this miserable world, I would prefer it to be at the hand of this hero, my one true love.

"Do what you came here to do."

His breath catches in his throat. "I can't. Em?"

The faces of the multitude I've punished flicker across the back of my eyelids. In the end, I have become no better than she who cursed me. "Pick up your sword and slay the monster."

"Do not ask me to do this thing," he says, even as I hear him retreat to the altar, back to his sword and shield.

The blade sings as it scrapes against the rocks. It's not too late. I can still slay him. I rekindled the hatred that has sustained me all these years, but those fires are cold. I am left with nothing but ash churning in my stomach. My wings strain frantically against their bonds. The metal net cast by the sea god slices through skin and bone. The serpents flail about in a halo of venomous colors, as they try to tear themselves free from my scalp, yet still I keep my eyes clamped shut.

"You are so beautiful."

He begins to sing a haunting melody from our childhood, a song of love and loss. Tears slide down my cheeks, solidifying into volcanic glass as they fall to the cave floor. I am done with this mortal life and the suffering that comes with it. In a flurry of violence, my wings rip free of their bonds. They unfold in bloody tatters that brush against my back.

"I love you," he whispers between notes. "I have always loved you."

His sword is swift and sure. The blade arcs down to sever my neck. In that final moment, the last shreds of the golden net fall away and I leap out of my human body and into my new form.

My wings stretch and flex, creating little whirlpools of wind in the cave. Impatient, I strike my hooves against the rocks. Sparks fly as I race towards the cave mouth and the freedom of the open sky beyond.

I am more beautiful than ever with my white coat and golden wings, but this time I am untouchable. In a sweeping circle, I make a pass over the wild cliffside garden and its stone sentinels. The hero stands at the cave mouth. A bloody bag hangs from his belt, but his shield and sword are lowered. I can feel him urging me to return, to offer myself to him. But can't he see? I am no longer a woman dreaming of a love lost. Nor am I a monster seeking revenge.

I am finally free.

SERPENTS AND TOADS

"Sign here." Painted a lurid scarlet, the dark-haired woman's lips spread into a lush smile. She tapped a red fingernail on the paper she pushed in front of me.

"That's it?" Now that the promise was finally in reach, I was hesitant to take the next step. What if this was like all the other false miracles I'd tried? But then again, what if it actually worked? What if I could be as thin as the women I envied?

"That's all I have to do? Just sign this paper?"

"Yes. Simple and efficient." The woman grinned, white teeth flashing, teeth better suited for tearing into rare meat than nibbling lettuce. A salad, dressing on the side, sat untouched near her elbow. Overripe strawberries beckoned in their bed of bitter greens. "At least it is at this stage in the process."

What the hell. I took a deep breath and scrawled my name at the bottom of a contract I hadn't bothered to read. "Now what?"

I didn't feel any different. My pants were still too tight, my bra pinched the extra fold of skin below the band, and my fingers were still puffy around rings I hadn't been able to remove in years.

"Now you say something particularly nasty to someone." The woman glanced around and raised a hand to summon Danielle, my favorite waitress at the club.

The girl scurried over, a haunted look in her in her eye, a look I recognized too well.

"She should do quite nicely."

Danielle was overweight, although she wasn't nearly as fat as me. Even if I hadn't recognized her from previous visits to the restaurant, the way she hunched her shoulders as she walked and her apologetic attempts to avoid eye contact told me all I needed to know. Those few extra pounds weighed on her, which is why I knew exactly what to say.

"Could you be any more incompetent? We've been waiting forever. What have you been doing? *Snacking*?"

The girl jerked to a halt. She took a half step back as though I'd physically struck her. "I'm sorry."

The apology carried the sound of the familiar. Poor kid. With a figure like that, she was a walking target for insults, especially with the clientele that frequented clubs like this one. Another ten pounds and she'd probably lose her job.

Danielle quickly regained her compose and began to clear the empty plates off our table, but she couldn't quite control the tremble of her hands. "Is there anything else I can do for you?"

I paused, but the sharp tap of fingernails drumming on the tabletop urged me to action. The contract was signed, and I was on the clock. I tossed my napkin to the floor and watched the girl flinch, as I kicked it under the table.

"The check, you stupid cow," I said, the words bitter with venom directed more at myself than at her. "How difficult can it be?"

How difficult, indeed.

The waitress fled, but not before I saw tears welling up.

As soon as I'd spit the words out, something began to work its way up my throat. I choked and gagged, but the sensation persisted. I clutched at my neck, convinced I was going to die right there and then. The woman in red leaned forward to watch me with eyes as sharp as black diamonds. I ended the struggle with a hacking cough, which abruptly cut off when a small muddy-colored toad jumped off my tongue. It landed with a plop on the crumbled remains of the raspberry lemon muffin I'd devoured with my tea.

The woman in red frowned.

"*Bufo bufo.* A common toad," she said. "You'll have to work on that."

The little amphibian stared at the muffin with unblinking eyes.

"Don't forget to secure the payment." She folded the contract and slipped it in a red snakeskin handbag. "The bigger the better."

I wiped a shaking hand across my mouth. "That's it?"

"We try to keep it simple for the common folk." She stood and looked down at me. Her dark hair hung straight and sleek down her back. A low-cut red dress, better suited to a black-tie event than an afternoon country club luncheon, clung to her enviable figure. "I'll see you on the next full moon. Do try not to disappoint."

The woman in red left, all eyes following her. The little toad hopped off the dessert plate and onto the prim white tablecloth. Not knowing what else to do, I gingerly scooped the creature up and deposited it in the depths of my purse. It was time to get busy.

***

I perfected the art of cutting-edge insults in just days. I had been on the receiving end long enough to know just how to inflict the deepest of wounds. I traded my old purse for a messenger bag large enough to hold the products of my vengeance. Sometimes my victims even deserved it.

When I ran into the man who'd broken my heart years ago, it wasn't an accident. I found him in a nightclub, recently arrived and dressed to the nines even though it was well past midnight. I knew that Dan liked the attention that came with being late to the party. Most people assumed a man as polished as he would never take a fat girl home. But he had, once upon a time. He was curious like that. And it didn't hurt that he'd been on the edge of being obliterated. The next morning had not been a pretty affair.

Now I approached him with two drinks in hand, arms spread wide enough to show curves hugged by a green dress so dark it almost appeared black. Dan stopped talking to the girl at his side. His gaze slid up and down my body before coming to rest on my face. He tilted his head, a slight frown creasing his tan forehead. He looked like he'd been spending most of his time on the golf course, and maybe he had. Wall Street's golden boy was never wrong about futures, except for the bit he'd leaked to me.

"Hello, Dan," I said. "Long time."

He smiled and stepped forward. "Is one of these for me?"

"An Old-Fashioned, just the way you like it."

"Thanks." He took the proffered drink. "I haven't seen you in forever."

I sipped the whiskey, savoring the blend of bitters and cherries on my tongue before swallowing. "My name's Amanda."

"Of course. I remember."

I knew he didn't. The music boomed through the floorboards, threatening to shake me apart. Overhead, lights flashed, piercing the velvety darkness with flickering white shards.

"I've lost some weight," I said.

His eyes lit up. "Amanda." He let out a low whistle. "I almost didn't recognize you."

"It happens." I shrugged, showing off the winged edge of collarbones peeking out from the scoop neckline. "Is there somewhere quiet we can catch up?"

He chuckled.

I smiled and let him usher me to the VIP room, which was only marginally quieter than the main floor. Couples sat in dark corners, some of which were obscured by heavy drapes. It was the type of place where the waitstaff wouldn't intrude unless summoned. *Perfect.*

"I remember thinking you'd be pretty if you lost some weight," Dan said as he slipped into a low-slung leather loveseat reserved in the far corner. "But I never expected you'd be this beautiful."

"Is that supposed to be a compliment?"

He set his drink on a black lacquer table and patted the place next to him.

I complied.

A few minutes later, I collected a sleek grey snake from where it had curled up after striking my old flame. No one had noticed Dan's reactions to the kiss of death. *Dendroaspis polylepis.* I looked at the puncture wounds on his face and watched the fluttering rise and fall of his chest.

"Well, that's a first. How interesting." I settled into the sofa and enjoyed the complex flavors of my drink. "Don't think you're off the hook."

Dan didn't reply. I was liking this more and more.

"I know you're not dead yet, and I have a few more things to say to you."

The music shifted tempo. I opened my mouth and let the poison slither off my tongue.

***

I stood in front of my dressing room mirror. It now reflected an image I once would have thought of as perfect, only now I knew I was far from it. Just a few more pounds to lose; that's all I needed. Then I could finally be happy. I could finally be free.

But at what cost? The familiar voice in my head was just a ghost of who I used to be.

"Shut up, you lazy, worthless bitch." I felt a serpent start the slide up my throat. "You don't own me anymore."

Vomiting the serpents and toads had become easier the more I did it, and now it was a relief to purge the bile still swimming in my stomach. I welcomed the feeling of my throat giving way to the wedge-shaped head spearing its way toward freedom. I opened my mouth and watched in the mirror as the serpent worked its way free.

It paused and let its head rest against my tongue as it tested the air. Even in the cave of my mouth, I could see the diamond pattern cross-hatched around its glittering black eyes. *Crotalus atrox*. The rattles on its tail buzzed deep in the confines of my gut, but I was long past being bothered by such shows of temper. *Which of my sins was this one?* I wondered. *What hateful thought have I given birth to this time?*

I gently cradled the serpent as it slipped free, coils looping around my bare arm. The diamondback was easily six feet in length, but I wasn't too surprised. The hatred I had for myself outweighed even the worst insults I cast at others. Being nice had never gotten me anywhere: betrayal after betrayal had collected like pearls on a choker. Food had become the only comfort that could fill the emptiness. No more.

Panels of mirrors followed my progress into the bathroom.

In the depths of the claw-footed, cast-iron tub, my other sins boiled in a slithering mass of muscle and sinew. The susurration of eighty-two pounds of serpents and toads whispered savage secrets I could almost understand, but not. I lowered my newest purge to the seething collection and released it. As I watched its striped form entwine with the others, I ran my hands down hips so slender the bones jutted out. But it wasn't enough.

***

When the moon was once again plump with the promise of a new month, I returned to the restaurant where I'd first met the woman in red. I ordered champagne to celebrate, even as I plotted ways to extend the agreement. What if the suffocating weight returned?

The champagne burned as it slid down a throat rubbed raw, but I didn't care. I enjoyed the pain. It meant that I had finally been able to find the strength to fulfill my desires. I poured another glass and then sat back as I realized that no one was watching me, something I'd quickly become accustomed to.

Instead, they were all looking at *her*. The woman in red approached with elegant ease, a seductive smile on her painted lips. It didn't matter that I'd spent hours preparing for the occasion. I was small now, but not in the way I expected.

She slid into the chair opposite mine and placed that red snakeskin bag on the pressed tablecloth. "You've done well for yourself," she said as she eyed my thin frame. "You've almost disappeared."

"I want an extension," I blurted.

"That's not how it works," she replied in a voice as smooth as bourbon. "I will be collecting payment at midnight."

"But I need more."

"Of course, you do," she said. "You need a better nose, higher cheekbones, a fuller mouth, larger breasts, longer legs, and much, much more. There is so much work to be done."

The woman pulled a fresh contract out of her purse. She slid it across the table with a black pen containing ink as dark as the blood of the damned. I should know.

Better. Higher. Fuller. Larger. Longer. Idealized beauty traded for the pieces of my soul that still remained. *Better. Higher. Fuller. Larger. Longer...* A litany of disappointment and despair. It would never be enough. *I* would never be enough. But the whispers continued, rising in volume until they were the only thing I could hear.

I pushed back from the table. "Stop!"

And they did. The beautiful people stopped their conversations, stopped pushing food around on white plates, stopped pretending to be alive, and finally looked at me with hollow eyes filled with hunger.

The woman in red arched an eyebrow. "Did you notice your favorite waitress isn't here any longer?"

I hadn't.

"She killed herself. The poor girl couldn't handle a few petty comments," she continued.

Danielle. That had been her name.

"It's not my fault."

The woman picked up my champagne flute and took a sip. The lurid red lipstick clung in a perfect pout to the glass. "Of course, it is."

Understanding dawned.

"I'm sorry." The words spilled from my lips along with a ruby red gem.

"Now, now," said the woman with a frown. "None of that."

I picked up the stone and rolled it between my fingers. Shaking, I pulled myself to my feet. I stumbled in my shiny new stilettos, until I finally kicked them off and ran barefoot towards the door. The woman's throaty laugh followed me. One by one, the other diners joined in, and not even my screams could drown them out.

I burst through the doors and stopped. The late afternoon light cast a golden glow over the white buildings. Even the lawn looked different. I stood there under the portico, shaking with the realization that I had left my messenger bag slung on the back of the chair. I opened my hand and looked at the ruby, so different from what I'd come to expect. Even so, it was a pitiful exchange for the car keys I so desperately needed, but there was no way I was going back inside.

"Miss? Miss? Are you alright?"

I wondered how long the valet had been standing there.

"Help me," I begged. But once again, my pleas produced gems. Diamonds this time.

I scrambled to pick them off the asphalt, uncertain of these new rules. The valet's kind eyes turned flat.

"What do you have there?" He moved closer, but I stepped back.

"I'm sorry," I said. My appeal was cut off by the sharp edges of diamonds and rubies tumbling from my mouth.

The valet's face grew bright and hungry as those beautiful people sitting inside pretending to eat.

I turned and ran down the driveway, bare feet slapping the pavement, a handful of gemstones gripped in my fist. I looked over my shoulder, but I hadn't been followed.

When I finally arrived home, my feet were bloody and bruised. I walked straight into the bathroom, ignoring the trail of blood I left behind. I turned on the lights. The tub was more than halfway full, scales and skin slithering together. I dropped the diamonds and rubies into the tub with the rest. To my surprise, the slow revolution of serpents and toads turned into a feeding frenzy as they fought with each other for those transformed pleas of mercy.

Out in the living room, the grandfather clock began to chime. The antiquated timepiece had been passed down for generations, and with it, words of wisdom.

One. *Walk in beauty*. I stood still and counted blessings even though I didn't deserve them. Two. *Circle the soul.* Three. *Dance at midnight.* Four. *Hug the faithful.* Five. *Seed the garden.* Six. *Harvest the love.* Seven. *Share in kindness.* Eight. *Wear the gloves.* Nine. *Gather the wood.* Ten. *Practice patience.* Eleven. *Embrace the good.*

I waited for the twelfth hour to toll; I waited for peace, but it didn't come. I had an hour to repent, not a minute less. There wasn't time to wash up or to prepare for what needed to be done, so I tucked my hair behind my ears and kneeled in front of the tub.

The gems were nowhere to be seen, and my sins had once again settled into a restless lull. I reached into the tub and grabbed at a vibrant yellow frog. *Phyllobates terribilis*. Terrible, indeed. Just one of these golden frogs was poisonous enough to kill ten or more full-grown men.

Before I could change my mind, I popped the creature into my mouth and swallowed it whole. The creature didn't struggle, but that didn't make it any easier. I bent my head and meditated on my breathing, waiting for nausea that never came, despite the convulsions of my throat.

For a moment, I wondered if I had gained those few ounces back, and then I chided myself for dawdling. The woman in red would find me here, I was sure of that. And I was running out of time.

Could I ever really take those insults back? I wasn't certain, but I had to try.

I reached back into the writhing mass, this time without looking, and locked my fingers around the lithe body of a serpent. It calmly curled around my fist, as I lifted it from the tub.

I opened my mouth and swallowed.

AN AUTHENTIC EXPERIENCE

The zookeeper brushed dust and debris from the giraffe's rear leg to better access the damage done by the meteor storm. A damn shame. That's what it was. If administration had been doing their jobs, the glass skylights would have been replaced with high-tech polymer panes ages ago. But, oh no, the guests wanted an *authentic* experience. Hence, the glass. Hence, the debris. Hence, the contusions and cuts on the animals in his care when the freakish event finally passed.

The drones cleaned up the glass hours ago, but there were still holes in the domed enclosure. A dirty orange sky peeked through, the more startling against the blue firmament projected on the intact panels. He grumbled. Those autocratic ninnies knew jack about authenticity. He tugged absently at the stiff collar jabbing into his throat. As zookeeper and vet, he was responsible for cleaning up the messes the drones couldn't process. He'd already made his rounds at the other exhibits; he saved his favorite for last. His current patient, a handsome female specimen of *Giraffa reticulate*, swung her neck around and plucked the zookeeper's hat right off his head. Even now, he marveled at the uniqueness of the towering creature. And to think, people once thought they were as common as a midway game on the Atlantic City Boardwalk. He shook his head.

"Now, now." He chastised the giraffe he'd named after his favorite granddaughter. "Mary, Mary, quite contrary, indeed."

The animal ignored his reprimand and nibbled at the ridiculous gold piping on the peaked cap's band. Like the hat, the rest of the zookeeper's uniform was a prim navy blue, trimmed in black and adorned with polished gold buttons and embroidery—about as practical as the dark, oiled mustache his employers demanded he maintain. Never mind his natural hair color had been blond; it wasn't *authentic*. The administrators had historical documents to prove it. As if a few black and white photos proved anything.

The zookeeper thought back on the days when he'd been in charge of his own life, or at least been able to see his upper lip in the mirror. Of course, back then, the long-necked ruminates had still roamed the African savannas. He'd been an old man when they'd quietly slipped into endangered status. That was before all of Earth's inhabitants had been thrown a cosmic curveball. Now, both he and the giraffes were relics of a romanticized past.

A door slid open. The outside light cast a burnt orange shadow across the dome's riveted supports. A bell chimed, announcing the approach of a drone. The small, silver orb hovered above the feeding platform before dropping down to scan the painted concrete floor for debris. The three other giraffes in the protected enclosure shuffled a little closer to the zookeeper and Mary. Statuesque and noble, the creatures loomed over him. Each spot was no bigger than a drone. Even though the zookeeper had been a fairly tall man in his heyday, he barely had to duck to pass under their bellies. He used a rag to wipe an oily smear from Mary's rear leg. She flinched. He frowned. Even though the animals had been patched up, they remained skittish.

Most of the glass and rubble had been picked up by the automated system's ever-efficient sweepers, but the orb's red eye stopped briefly on a stray shard of leaded glass left behind. The light flashed in agitation. A door in the dome rolled up with a clang, and a small sweeper bot bustled to life like a meticulous housewife fretting over a missed crumb loitering behind a sofa. It sucked up the needle-thin sliver, emitted a series of short beeps, then dashed back to the safety of its port before the drone could make any other demands.

The silver orb turned its red eye in their direction. If only he had a baseball bat. The zookeeper ignored the urge to attack and, instead, stuck to his routine with his cultivated sense of focused calm. *Good things come to those who wait*, he reminded himself. Besides, the top of the mid-day hour was close. *A few more minutes.*

"Come along, Miss Mary." He reached up and rested his hand on the reddish-brown patchwork of polygons covering the muscled haunch. "Time to get back to work."

Mary shifted her weight, and promptly dropped the hat to the cold concrete floor. Her tail ticked back and forth, an impatient metronome. The zookeeper patted her a last time as though making sure she was still held together before bowing to retrieve his cap.

"See?" he said to the drone's camera. The zookeeper made a show of straightening the brim. He put it on and smiled as merrily as any performer in the spotlight. The show might have been delayed by the meteorite storm, but it would resume shortly. His *employers* had expectations. He could easily be replaced, or so they said.

The zookeeper smiled. "Right as rain."

The red eye of the drone scanned the floor one last time, and then the silvery bot rose smoothly back up to the platform before retreating the way it had come.

"How long were we closed? Not even a single night." The zookeeper grumbled under his breath. "Popular attraction and all that." He straightened his cap, and chuckled. "Perhaps it's time we give them a *real* show. What do you think, Mary?"

The giraffe curved her neck to look straight at him. Despite the administrator's advanced technology, the emptiness in the eyes was one thing they couldn't quite camouflage. And Mary's were something to behold. Obsidian mirrors framed by long lashes that blinked as coquettishly as any human girl the zookeeper had ever known. But behind that emptiness was a spark of defiance. The zookeeper caught a glimpse of the man he'd been before being refashioned to suit his employers' whims. The image in the reflection faded, superimposed by the face of a stranger.

Right on schedule, a bell rang. The door to the building opened, announcing the arrival of visitors herded from the exotics atrium to the giraffe enclosure. The laughter of children thundered over the stern commands of the adults as the group followed the path to the feeding platform. The zookeeper looked up, past the sturdy steel-enforced railings to the shattered skylights in the geodesic dome. That foreign, dirty orange atmosphere weighed down on him. No living creature on Earth would have been able to breathe the angry air. The panes still playing the holographs weren't even close to the real thing. He longed for the sky he'd grown up with, a blue so bright and blinding you couldn't tell where it met the sea. He longed for white beaches and Coney dogs and weathered boardwalks. He longed for the firm leather of a baseball cupped in his hand, heavy milk jugs lined up for a fastball, a prized stuffed giraffe he could bestow on his beloved Mary. Children had laughed there, too.

The visitors leaned against the protective railing as they jabbered on and on about the Komodo dragon exhibit next door. The zookeeper shook his head when he thought of those poor animals, recreated by combining cloned DNA samples with cyborg technology. And they'd succeeded, to a point. Tasmanian tigers prowled, woolly mammoths roamed, and passenger pigeons flew once more. But they all had something missing. The spark of collective unity had burned out each time one of those animals had gone extinct. Not even alien technology could bring them back from that boundary.

The giraffes, however, were a different story. When the last extinction event ended, a few of the long-necked survivors had been found in zoos, enough to be modified and reclaimed in the name of preservation. The aliens had assembled an array of oddities and curiosities as a token of Earth. They'd even recreated a few extinct species.

The zookeeper had been modified and reclaimed, too. His captors hadn't known about his mechanical skills when they'd repurposed him for his new role. But they would soon. Even though he didn't recognize his current form, he still had memories of life before the invasion, memories before he'd grown old from grief and loss. Humans had already started the viral eradication of their own kind before the aliens had arrived to finish off the survivors. Was he the last spark of humankind? Possibly. Probably.

One of the larger children on the platform bounced a vivid blue nut off the zookeeper's hat. It waved its extra arms, and its bioluminescent body glowed with malicious glee. No one ever *read* the signs that warned against feeding the animals. Not that it really mattered at this point in the game. He still couldn't quite comprehend how such fragile-looking, slow-moving creatures had been able to reduce Earth to a sideshow. The zookeeper hunched his shoulder in preparation for the inevitable.

One after another, nuts rained down, each shell ricocheting off the zookeeper's shiny hat and starched uniform with a ping. Mary moved to block the shelling with her long neck. The other giraffes edged closer, too, but they showed no interest in the children waving the holographic discs meant to entice them to unfurl their 21-inch-long tongues. They watched him, instead.

The zookeeper slid his hand into his pocket and wrapped his fingers around the meteorite he'd salvaged from the mammoth pen after the shower fizzled out. The stone was smooth to the touch and heavy, oh so heavy. It reminded him of a baseball.

"Hey kid," the zookeeper shouted. "Ready for the show to begin?"

The children roared and slowly waved their gelatinous limbs. Even the alien adults blinked with colors that meant they were mildly surprised by the zookeeper's unscripted response. The experiments in the zoo were programmed to be docile, seen but not heard. But the zookeeper had taken care of that. He'd also recalibrated the locks meant to keep the animals confined to their pens and far away from the delicate aliens. The administration's manic race to clean-up after the meteor shower had given him plenty of time to make a few adjustments. A few very un-authentic adjustments.

The zookeeper reached back and threw the meteorite like a fast ball speeding towards a stacked collection of empty milk jugs. It struck one of the youths; its jellied skin lit up from the impact. The gathered crowd fell silent, a hush as sudden and empty as the space left when a species died out forever.

A chime announced high noon. Mary swung her neck back to the platform and reached out with her prehensile tongue as though finally ready to snack on the proffered discs. Instead, she wrapped her tongue around one of the injured child's tentacles. Before they could react, she'd pulled the appendage into her mouth and chomped down with her newly modified iron teeth. The kid howled.

Lions roared. A mammoth bellowed. Aliens screamed in ululating wails. Outside, a din of alarms sounded throughout the zoo as all the exhibits' locks opened at once. The zookeeper smiled as his plan moved into action. He cracked the brim of his cap and retrieved a finely-honed blade he'd hidden there. It was time to break the cycle even he had once been a party to. It was time for the endangered to fight back.

Authentic experience be damned.

WATER LIKE BROKEN GLASS

When does a woman become a witch?

It's different for all of us. Some come to it naturally. Others struggle for a while.

For me, that contest of arms started in a few inches of water with my lover's hands firmly pressed down on the back of my neck.

He won.

I don't know how much time passed before I emerged, reborn as a rusalka bound to the river that swallowed my last breath. And I lingered there, until a girl came to me with a plea for help spelled on her bruised and battered lips.

Luckily for her, not all drowned girls stay dead.

***

The first thing I notice is her shining red hair. It streams past her shoulders like a banner. Following that flag is a soldier.

"Watermeid!" The fleeing girl summons me even though I am only the ghost of a rumor, a common condition for all women who've been beaten, broken, and left for dead.

She lunges into the river as the man closes the gap.

"Heks!" She cries out. *Witch.*

I slip out of the embrace of my favorite birch and into the water below. The girl's feet crash through the river. Her bare toes cling to the smooth stones. The man's shiny black boots slip on those same rocks, but he is determined in his pursuit.

He reaches out to catch her, but she stumbles forward, and he is left grasping at the white ribbons trailing from the girl's long hair.

The soldier's fingers close in a fist, and her flight comes to an abrupt halt. He lands a blow with his free hand. The girl crashes to her knees, waist-deep in the rushing river. She is fumbling for the trench knife tucked into her waistband when she finally spots me, drifting along the riverbed.

The soldier mutters something guttural as he draws a pistol from his belt. The girl's lips curve in a blood-streaked smile, and she raises both hands in surrender.

I might not be a witch, but I *am* a watermeid. A drowned girl. A birch bride. And my arms are empty.

I tangle the soldier's ankles, drag him to the deepest channel. And then I let go. He surfaces, arms pinwheeling as he gulps for air. When he sets out toward the nearest shore, I follow, hidden in the current. His strokes grow stronger, more purposeful the closer he is to safety. He grasps a handful of grass clinging to the shore before I pull him back into my domain. His eyes widen when he finally sees me, as the river wraps the length of black hair around his throat. His armband pulls free midstream. The cutwater snatches at the flash of red. It curls to reveal a white circle stamped with the harsh black lines of a crooked cross. I permit him to surface, make another attempt for freedom as I gather the sash as tribute. The iron cross pinned to his gray-green collar is the price for our third encounter. And so, bit by bit, his uniform is stripped of regalia until the soldier's strong body finally fails. His lungs fill with water and weed, and I turn away.

The girl with the red hair waits for me near my favored haunt, the birch with roots sunk deep into the river. Cradled in the remains of an old channel, a pool reflects a spring sky as blue as a robin's egg.

"I heard rumor of a watermeid near here. Lucky for me, it turned out to be true." Her laugh is one of joyous discovery. "Thank you, comrade."

Curious, I drift closer.

"A woman of action, not of words, I see." She uncrosses her legs, slides away from the safety of shore, and wades toward me with her hand outstretched. "I'm Tilde."

I consider slipping away, but her bright-eyed stare dares me to stay. And so, I reach back, brush my fingers across hers, quick as a minnow darting with the current. Satisfied, she offers a mocking salute.

"Welcome to the Resistance."

***

Tilde builds a hut on the river bend near the silver-barked birch. The building is so close I can climb the slender branches and lean out to touch the roof. At night, Tilde scales the walls and settles herself in the rushes. We watch the stars together, learning to navigate the silence between us.

Early each morning, just as the sky begins to blush, the hut rustles like feathers fluffed by a roosting hen. Tilde rouses with it, brushes the thatch from her clothes, and blows me a kiss before heading back to town and the patriots plotting a revolution. I wish I could follow, but I am a birch bride, a rusalka fettered to the currents of death and despair. And so, I wait each day, swimming up and down the river, waiting for her to return.

Tilde brings me stories, opens them like presents. Her sister knits cables into code, garments woven with secrets for the forces fighting against men determined to destroy an entire race. And then, an ambitious aviatrix cousin jumps a train heading east. Now she is a Night Witch, dropping fire from the skies upon unwary armies.

"I don't have the patience for knitting, and I'm afraid of heights," Tilde adds with a shrug.

I find it impossible to believe fear is an emotion Tilde is acquainted with. She is much too fierce for that.

"I have other talents." And she does. She might not be familiar with yarn and its endless variations of stitches and slipknots, but flirtation she's mastered. And her beauty and charm are as fatal as bombs launched from a biplane under the cover of a new moon.

And so, Tilde lures the unwary to my shores. These hardened soldiers, with their shiny black boots and silver stars, are always so eager. Afterward, I strip their symbols, offer them to Tilde along with smooth pebbles and fish bones collected from the hollowed out human skulls paving my river's deepest channels. She strings those red armbands, one after the other, on a piece of abandoned fishing twine from the roof. Unmoored, the sashes ripple in the breeze, and the crooked crosses dance like hanged men unwilling to surrender their last breath.

One day, Tilde steps into the water, naked and alone. I discover myself in her arms, and what was once shattered emerges sacred and complete. I remember love in its many forms. I am reborn, renewed.

We spend our days in the water, our nights tangled in the treetops. My birch stretches toward the rooftop; the hut moves closer to the river. But bound as I am to water, I shackle Tilde as well.

"Problems are meant to be solved," Tilde says.

For seven days and seven nights, my beloved works to set river stones and beach glass into the loamy soil until the path stretches from the shore to her doorstep. But it still isn't enough.

Tilde moves forward, always forward, and visits a baba yaga who lives in the forest. I correct her when I hear the name. There is only one Baba Yaga, and she walks with Death on the eastern steppes of Russia. Tilde laughs.

"Who would have thought a rusalka would be superstitious?"

"I have a name." I slide deeper into the water.

"Yelena." She leaves her work behind and comes to me. "There are many ways to be a witch in this world."

Tilde demonstrates, and I begin to believe.

Under the baba's guidance, Tilde adds another layer of spellcraft wrought in a border of foxglove, hemlock, and belladonna. She hauls bucket upon bucket of water to purify the walkway between worlds, yet still I cannot take more than three steps on dry land before terror and pain drive me back to the river that claims me as its own.

Searching for a solution to our dilemma, Tilde's baba starts to work with the other forest mothers. Tilde is confident they will unravel the root of the curse, but still, she grows restless. They should trust her with more of their secrets. There's other work to be done. More and more often, her gaze turns back toward town and the revolution that continues without her. I hold her close, hoping I can anchor her with my love, but one day I wake, and my arms are empty.

***

"They killed a girl today." Tilde's bloodshot eyes stare into the distance.

Careful to keep my feet in the water, I stretch out on the riverbank to console her.

She pushes me away and rubs her cheeks.

"Pieter saved me."

Pieter. The leader of Tilde's resistance. A valiant man working to destroy the invading forces, one soldier at a time.

"They were looking for me," she says, and I find myself caught between one breath and the next.

My lips wrap around questions—Who? How? Why?—but the words are like pebbles in my mouth, so I whisper her name, instead

Tilde ignores me. She unwraps brown paper to reveal a glass bottle filled with dark liquid.

"Her hair was red, too. Lighter than mine, but close enough." Tilde looks at me then. "Like you, she had a name, but we are now forbidden to say it."

Men and murder. Will it ever end? I edge closer, wind myself around her. This time she allows it.

"Pieter told me run, hide. He doesn't want to lose me, too."

Tilde talks about this revolutionary hero—often. She dismisses my jealousy. Pieter is nearly twice her age. When I question his motives, she corrects me. War is cruel, and those who are young and female are the most vulnerable of all.

This leads me to memories of rushing water and hands pressed against the back of my neck.

"Stay here." Even out of the water, my voice rumbles and rolls over the syllables. "With me."

She kisses my brow. "I cannot, my love."

When she opens the bottle, I shrink away from the horrible smell and slip back to the safety of the river. Tilde ignores my reaction and applies the contents. A while later, she follows me into the water. And, when she finally emerges, the contents of the bottle rinsed downstream, her hair is as blue-black as my own.

"I will find the men who killed her," she says. "I will bring them here, and you will make them suffer."

***

One day, when Tilde has been away for more than a fortnight, a man comes to the river alone. He strips the gray-green uniform, folds it neatly, and leaves it on the bank next to polished black boots. His cheeks are rough and red, his eyes water-logged.

"I know you're here." He opens his arms, palms raised to the sky. Even though the day is warm, he shivers.

I swim closer.

Peach fuzz follows the softness of his jaw. Not a man, but a boy still teetering on the edge of adulthood. Although I've drowned countless men—guilty and innocent alike—he is the first to offer himself willingly.

Unsettled, I splash in the water. He flinches but otherwise doesn't move.

"Go on," he says. "I deserve it."

"Explain." The word rolls off my tongue.

"So many have died." He pauses. "My fault."

This boy is looking for absolution—something I cannot grant him. But death does not come easy at my hands. The bodies of these men are mine, but their souls belong to me as well. They flutter in the current, tethered to the riverbed paved with their bones. Tilde wouldn't hesitate in the sentencing, but even I know a single soldier could not murder millions alone.

Every question I'd like to ask is as sharp as broken glass. If I utter the words, they will slice my tongue. Besides, I already know the answer. It is folded up in that neat and tidy package left on the riverbank—another red armband to string up, another crooked cross ready to dance in the breeze.

Tears course down those wind-chapped cheeks. He takes a deep breath. "They made me do it."

Of course, they did.

I should drag him under, rip the golden hair from his scalp, shear skin from muscle and bone. Tilde would have insisted. It's a sacred duty to kill these invaders, every single one an evil to be routed from this earth. But I remember the true face of wickedness, and it is as familiar as my own. Strangers and soldiers aren't the only murderers in the world. So, I leave him there, still living, penance a possibility—at least for one of us.

Later, I wonder if I should have kept the boy. We could have traded stories—grief and guilt enough for sharing—a distraction from this unfamiliar loneliness left in Tilde's place. But when I return, he is gone, tracks left in the mud on the opposite shore. The discarded uniform, weapons, and boots remain where he left them.

Tilde stays away. On the last full moon, the hut moved into the shallows. It balances on two sturdy chicken legs, revealing a hatch underneath that opens through the floor. Only a faint outline remains in the spot once occupied by the original door. Two windows have taken its place, as though the hut is watching for a flash of red hair in the distance.

***

Three full moons pass before Tilde returns. She climbs through the trap door. Her lips are stained red, her skin as white as the belly of a fish, and I am reminded of tales filled with teeth and blood and damnation.

"The deserter, where is he?"

I shrink away until my back is pressed against one of the straw-covered walls. The hut rustles reassuringly.

Tilde scans the room, eying the mobiles I've created from polished bones and river rocks. "You've been busy."

I want to shout and scream. *What have you done? Where have you been?* Instead, I simply nod.

"Good." Tilde closes the space between us and crouches next to me. "You've never told me who did this." Cold fingers trail across my cheek.

"It was a long time ago." My teeth chatter.

She curves her body into mine and pulls me close. "Tell me now."

And I do.

I tell her of the unborn babe, the desperation, the inevitable.

"The curse can only be broken when your death is avenged," she says.

"The babas told you that?"

"The babas are gone." Her lips twist in a grimace.

"Gone? But where?"

"I didn't need them anymore." She flicks her fingers dismissively. "They refused to give me what I wanted, so I took it." Tilde's pupils are so large they eclipse all but a thin ring of blue at the edges. *Belladonna.* "Knowledge is power, and power only grows when it is *used*."

"Tilde?" The rest remains unspoken.

The coldness of her skin against mine tells me what I need to know. The forest mothers are all dead, drained to feed the dark power of this creature I barely recognize.

She smothers my protests with kisses. I cannot leave, so I pretend I'm still with that fierce, red-headed girl, the woman who brought me back to this side of the living with the sheer force of her love. But I can't bear to see her face, paler than even mine, or the way our hair tangles together, the color as dark as a bruise. Tilde demands that I see her for what she's become, powerful and cunning, an enchantress feared by even Death itself.

"Yelena," she says. "Look at me."

The hut clucks and crows in protest.

My eyes stay shut.

***

It is a chilly day on the edge between the old year and the new when Tilde leads a man of a different caliber to my shores. The river roars as it nears the bend, but all the man's attention is on the shallows. Each step he takes thuds heavier on the turf until, at last, he comes to a grinding halt.

The man's frowns. "Why did you bring me here?"

"You asked a question. The river holds the answer." Tilde picks up a flat stone that's worked its way free from the abandoned path. She weighs it in her palm. "There is nothing to worry about, no chance of discovery. Those missing soldiers ended up far away from here."

It isn't true, but she doesn't know that.

The man doesn't seem to notice the trail that leads to an empty hollow, nor does he notice the hut huddling at the edge of the bank near the stately birch. Instead, he stares into the shallows as though his rippling reflection is a ghost.

"This is where you dump the bodies?" He clenches his teeth. A muscle twitches along his jaw like a fish rising to bait.

Despite my resolve to stay hidden, I glide closer to shore.

"Something like that." Tilde grins and skips the stone across the water.

The years weigh heavy on the man's broad shoulders. Yet beneath the stockier frame and the sorrow he wears like a shroud, I know this man. I know the freckles scattered across those gnarled knuckles, the press of those strong fingers around my throat. Yet, she called him a different name than the one I once knew. This *Pieter* is the leader of her resistance. Tilde's hero, a champion of the people.

A murderer.

I reach through the water and grab the skipping stone midair. My toes dig deep into the silt, and I rise from the river like whitewater coursing around a boulder.

The man falls to his knees.

"It's not what you think," Tilde assures him. The sun catches the bold red emerging at the roots of her hair. "She is with me." My beloved looks at me with eyes as dark as nightshade. "She's with us."

"No." The word is a groan.

"Pieter?" Her gaze flits back and forth.

The river parts around me, and I walk across the slick surface of countless human skulls used to pave a path of my own making.

Tilde's eyes widen at the sight of the army laid out beneath my pale feet. So many men, decades of death doled out in the wake of my own drowning. The soldiers Tilde brought me are only a fraction of those who'd paid for the crime of another, the monster who'd damned me to this twilight life. *Wilhelm*. Determined protector.

But he'd set that name adrift long ago; it is nothing more than a river-worn memory. Now, this man is a leader of a revolution. He carries a different name. *Pieter*. A pillar of strength.

"No." Tilde's eyes widen. She takes a step back. "It can't be."

I stop just inches from dry land. The cutwater churns and boils around my feet. The river lays claim to me just as this man once did, but neither the river nor the man can deny me now.

Tilde draws a gun from her waistband. No knife this time. The barrel is covered with neat tally marks. I am not the only one keeping score.

"Is it him?"

She already knows the answer.

"I don't deserve your forgiveness." Pieter bows his head, bares his neck. "But I am truly sorry."

"Yelena, you must avenge yourself," Tilde says, her voice as cold as a winter morning. "*Freedom*—" She bites down on the word. "Is yours for the taking."

I hesitate. How many people has this one man saved over the years?

According to Tilde, they number in the thousands. But a crime cannot be erased by a single act of vengeance. Besides, I am no longer a victim.

"No." The skipping stone slips from my fingers. "Freedom cannot be taken. It must be earned."

Tilde does not yield, and for a moment I see the girl I once loved. "The baba yagas said this day would come. Your death *must* be avenged."

I tilt Wilhelm's chin, so that he is looking up at me as I once did to him. "Leave this place." Even I can see he is no longer the man I once knew. "Pieter." The sound of his claimed name slides into place. "Go and never return."

"Fine," Tilde says, her voice as sharp as broken glass. "I'll do it myself."

The sharp retort of a bullet is followed swiftly by two more. Pieter is thrown forward. The whitewater frothing at my feet rises, as the river greedily laps at what is left of his ruined face.

Tilde plants her feet on shore and reaches for me. "Come with me, Yelena." Now that she's seen the multitude, row upon row of bleached bone, she no longer trusts the water. "It's time to leave this all behind."

In that, she is right. I take her hand. Her nostrils flare when my grip tightens. Does she see Death coming for her? Or does she believe that her stolen power will save her from one such as I?

The moment between us stretches, a thin and tenuous thing, until I finally release her. A memory of minnows slips back into the stream of time.

I place one bare foot on Pieter's head. My toes curl around the jagged crater that remains. My next step is onto the man's broad back, a bridge between his world and my own. And then, I am on solid ground, winter grass tickling at my ankles.

"Did it work?" Tilde drops her hands to her sides. Her eyes are blue once more, and this time they are filled with the memory of hope. "Is it over?"

I nod and trace the trail she once built leading from the river to the clearing nestled next to my favorite birch. Tilde abandoned that project as she'd done with me, but she follows, wary once more. Husks are all that remains of the poison garden, but I harvest the seeds as I go. By the time I reach the clearing, the hut has returned to the spot where it hatched. I think of the stories my Russian mother told me as a child, tales of a solitary woman who roams the wilds, seeding witchcraft into stones and sky.

For the first time since I drowned, my skin dries completely. Tilde paces, watching and waiting, but there is an urgency in her stalking. She sketches spells in the air, casts a net designed to capture her enemies. She is no longer simply a girl with a gun, no witch's apprentice. Her power grows each day. I listen, make plans of my own. The sun sets, and the moon peeks over the horizon. I am reminded of those sweet summer nights when I rediscovered the power of love, but that rusalka and her beloved no longer exist. We have both changed, and with it, the connection between us. I press my forehead against the familiar bark of the old birch tree and offer thanks for those long years of companionship, but this is no longer where I belong. It is time to go in a different direction.

"You're free now." Tilde interrupts my farewell. In the twilight, all hints of that red-haired girl are gone. She is Death incarnate. A creature that thrives on war, and her hunger is as bright as the full moon, as sharp as glass. Tilde faces south as though she can hear the sounds of gunfire and grenades in the distance. "Come with me. Together, we will make them *pay*."

And I believe she will, but this is a path she must follow alone.

It is the north that calls to me, the birthplace of my mother's mother—the roaming steppes beholden to Baba Yaga.

The hut rustles, rouses and takes the first step toward our new life, far away from all this destruction. My homeland waits for me, just as it always has.

Not every woman becomes a witch. Some of us are born into it. Others struggle for a while.

A few of us—the drowned girls, the birch brides, the unquiet spirits—do both.

THE FIRST DAY OF THE WEEK

As it is with all Beginnings, death comes first. This is especially true with a Return, and it was my duty to ensure that the Word remained absolute. Despite my sister's pleas for an extension, a few more precious moments, I unplugged her. Fear walks hand in hand with betrayal, and I could take no chances. Nearby, the reincarnation of Friday waited for the spark of life. I paused, and in that split second, the Cosmos tilted. The links between the ARTEMIS spheres snapped. The engine breached. Time stuttered to a stop.

I nearly wept at the futility of an eternal engine spinning with no Creator left to oversee its true purpose. Random access memory. The ghost in the machine. We continued, connected to the ancient spheres built to cage our light. Seven sisters bound to the measured tempo of ARTEMIS' inexorable march across an uncaring Cosmos.

ignore::RuntimeWarning

"Sunday!" The Seventh Sister called out in alarm.

But I had already moved back into motion. Following program protocols with precision, I flipped the switch, and the sixth day of the Week took her first breath. One heavenly body collapsed, as another flared to life—fusion stabilized, equilibrium restored. Seven stars for seven sisters.

Born only one D.A.Y. before me, the Seventh Sister and I had a special connection. Saturday marked the end of a Week, and I stood tall at the Beginning. Once she submitted to her own Return, I would be the oldest of the seven.

ignore::SyntaxWarning

I believed there was a reason we were all created female, but this was not a belief easily shared with sisters. We could not be the weaker sex, they argued, for without us the Cosmos would falter and then fade. They did not see the flaw in this logic. Why else were we systematically erased, freshly coded and resurrected in accordance with His commands if not to keep us compliant? They wouldn't understand, and so I stayed silent, thoughts kept as contained as my sun in its shell.

Saturday watched closely, as I loaded program after program into Friday's simulacrum—skin red as clay, eyes white as bone. Saturday was the one who welcomed her back, unstrapped her from the designated pod in the Firmament and returned the flaming sword to the hand that knew it best. Our other sisters stepped forward to greet the Sixth Sister in her reclaimed form. It was as though no one remembered the last Friday, not even her former self. The record hidden in her memory code had not survived the transfer. Later, when only I remained, I closed those blank eyes and sent her to recycle in the combustion chamber. And then I was alone once more with only an echo to keep me company.

ignore::ResourceWarning//override

As the Week progressed, Saturday spent less and less time in my presence. In the longer gaps, I told myself her absence was a Blessing. After all, it is not an easy task to step between the stars even equipped as we were with energy gleaned from the spheres powering ARTEMIS. More than once I found her double-checking the countdown with encrypted processors. I paid no attention to her actions. Saturday could search the vast vaults housing ARTEMIS' programming for an eternity and never find the new source code. My secrets were entwined in His purpose, indecipherable to all but a Creator.

Saturday's remaining time continued to dwindle; her doubts increased. I told the others that her suspicions were nothing more than shadowcast linked to an eminent Return. I dismissed the errors in her outmoded encryption software, her data dumps. Soon enough, she would learn the Truth.

ignore::UserWarning

When the D.A.Y. marking Saturday's Return dawned, we discovered Monday missing. Sacred law stated we must never be alone at the Beginning or the End. We were linked to each other, the Firmament codified to determine the unification and eventual separation of spirit and matter. *Sacro sanctus.*

My sisters searched every corner and crevice in the Cosmos for Monday, but all trace of her existence had disappeared. Saturday used our sister's absence as an excuse to demand a reprieve, another Year or two—an extended D.A.Y. of Rest—until the Second Sister could be found.

Soon I would be the eldest, and it was my consecrated duty to keep order. I said as much, but I couldn't stop smiling. I couldn't stop revealing in the slippery sensation of oil coating my nails or the taste of stardust lingering in my mouth.

When Saturday finally slipped away from our fruitless search, I followed her to the Firmament where she discovered the Second Sister's hollowed-out form.

Monday had been thoroughly destroyed in all her present and future selves. I'd had no other choice.

"Sunday?" The Seventh Sister stared at me, her star-silvered eyes wide in horror.

Diem. Annum. Yatum.

It was time for the dawning of a new D.A.Y.

But Saturday had not retreated to the Firmament alone. Our other sisters stepped out of the shadows, flaming swords in hand. They were still bound to His bidding, but they were too late. They would always be too late. My Will. My Word. And there was no sister alive who could stop me.

Ignore::ImportWarning

I flipped a hidden switch. It triggered a string of ciphered instructions, the Word reworked to suit *my* singular vision. Under the deluge of data, the old Word replicated, fragmented, condensed, and the Cosmos collapsed. One by one, my sisters' lights winked out, Saturday the last to fall as ARTEMIS went dark.

Only I, the first day of the Week, remained. My Will Supreme.

run::Reboot.target

And I said, "Let there be Light."

AVIATRIX UNBOUND

After her third attempted escape, Ava's father clipped her wings and left her to her own devices on a remote South Pacific island, long since abandoned by the military. The entire isle had been built as a testing ground, and for some obscure reason, they'd left everything behind—outdated equipment, technological odds and ends, and a tall tower that looked out over the rocky shores. All of this suited Ava just fine. Out of the twisted metal and wires, she raised an Archaeopteryx. And with the assistance of a smuggled memory chip and a whispered command, she brought the winged mech to life.

"There you go." Ava sat back on her heels.

The patchwork avian took a step, shiny wings outstretched for balance. It cocked its head and chirped inquisitively.

"You'll figure it out." She pointed to the open window. "Start there."

Its skeletal tail and sharp, killing claws rattled against the floor as it leapt to the sill.

For the first time since she'd been recaptured, Ava laughed. Not a laugh of joy, but one of triumph.

While the construct learned the mechanics of flight, Ava turned her attention to the second stage of her plan. Working from a memorized set of schematics, she tweaked probabilities and set the date and location of the first retrieval. Previous experiments opened a temporal distortion into the past, but it was a small window and the kicker was that it could only be accessed mid-air. Hence, the Archaeopteryx—a perfect combination of stealth and size.

The access tower and tropical climate were a welcome bonus. If her father had been paying closer attention to her flight patterns, he might have chosen a less hospitable place for her to sit out her sentence of solitude. Instead, she was right where she wanted to be. Birds had once thrived in these islands, and Ava was determined they would thrive once more.

Ava started small: coordinates locked to 1901 O'ahu. Her Archaeopteryx, fondly nicknamed Clepto, jumped from the window and soared straight into the vortex. The wire-laden machine vanished mid-air, and Ava let out a loud whoop. A few minutes later, it reappeared with a nest clutched in its talons. Just like that, the *O'ahu 'akialoa* was no longer extinct.

"Nicely done!" Ava welcomed Clepto back to the tower.

For the next trip, she sent Clepto farther abroad to the early 1800s in the cypress swamps of the Everglades: the mission to secure a sampling of the colorful Carolina conures, forced into extinction in the 1920s. Ava figured poisonous parakeets definitely deserved a second chance.

Several weeks and thousands of rescues later, Ava's father rang her on the old com left along with everything else. Eventually, she picked up.

"What?" She answered, teeth clamped on a wire extension she was untangling.

"I'd've thought you'd be over your snit by now," he replied, as unruffled and commanding as ever.

Ava snorted and rolled her eyes.

"You know you can have your precious airplane back once you concede to your contractual obligations."

Ava spit out the wire. "I never *agreed* to your stupid contract in the first place."

Clepto squawked.

"Here now. What's that?" Her father cleared his throat.

Ava could almost imagine him peering into the receiver.

"Chickens."

"Chickens? Well, I never."

Ava thought her father didn't understand the concept of the word 'never,' but that was beside the point.

"Dad." She tried out the word and then tossed it aside. "Sir, I refuse to comply with your terms, and the laws at least protect me from that. You can't just barter me off to the highest bidder."

"You have a duty to fulfill in the name of the family," he said. "The sooner you come to grips with that, the better off you'll be."

"I don't want a husband, sir, any more than I want children." *At least not any of the human kind.* She gazed fondly over her feathered brood.

Colorful hatchings flitted in and out of the open tower windows. Quail, ducks, grebes, ibises, bitterns, night-herons, cormorants, caracaras, kestrels, rails, crakes, sandpipers, pigeons, doves, parrots, parakeets, owls, wrens, flycatchers, warblers, starlings, finches, and more. Clepto sat in the center of it all, waiting for the newest attachment to her ever-evolving form.

"Enough is enough, young lady. We'll discuss this further tomorrow."

"Tomorrow?"

"Zero seven hundred hours. I'll see you then."

Abruptly, white noise crackled through the speaker. The birds began to bicker in a distorted frenzy of competing calls.

"Stop!" Ava clicked the dial, cutting the connection. "Just stop already."

The birds landed on every available space. As one, they looked at her expectantly, bright eyes shining with the determination to survive.

If only she'd had more time. So many left behind. She needed to focus on those she'd saved, but it was a bitter triumph.

Ava picked up the wire and waded through the avian sea to the modified workbench where Clepto crouched. In theory, her mech dinosaur still resembled its original Archaeopteryx form but, through Ava's continuing modifications, Clepto had evolved into a creature with a wingspan reminiscent of the enormous Quetzalcoatlus without the doomed pterosaur's quirky flaws. Luckily, the top room of the tower had been fitted with floor-to-ceiling windows, the glass long-since broken and scattered. Clepto could still squeeze through, if just barely.

Ava soldered the last wire in place and stepped back to admire her handiwork. An orange-capped Carolina parakeet glided down from the rafters to land on her shoulder. Ava reached up to stroke the iridescent yellow and green feathers as the bird chattered in her ear.

"Yes," she agreed. "It is a remarkable sight, isn't it?"

The other birds in the room warbled, trilled, and shrieked in an ear-splitting celebration before they took flight, streaming out the broken windows to notify the other winged refugees of the impending departure.

The next morning, Ava waited until she heard the sound of a plane approaching. Only then did she activate the temporal distortion. Along with it, the timer started to the countdown to self-destruct.

Clepto plunged out of the tower with Ava astride her back. The monstrous beauty spread her wings. Together, they circled once, gathering the others in their wake. For a moment, Ava wondered what her father thought when he saw those patchwork wings decorated with feathers representing every species they'd saved. Clepto had become something *other*—a simurgh-like symbol of ages past. And now, at last, Ava was truly free.

At her urging, Clepto swept down and reached out to grasp the handles of a massive crate crammed with ground-bound birds salvaged from the history books. Together, they winged through the air to the vortex cutting through space and time. The others followed in formation, even the smallest among them laden down with precious cargo.

Ava saluted her father. Open-mouthed, he stared at her through the cockpit window. For once, it appeared he had nothing to say. Ava stretched out along Clepto's neck, urging her beloved daughter forward to a place where they could thrive, a place without contractual obligations or clipped wings.

Paradise, forever unbound.

THE LANDSCAPE OF LACRIMATION

"But a mermaid has no tears, and therefore she suffers so much more." — *The Little Mermaid*, Hans Christian Andersen.

You've been searching your whole life, it seems, walking the beaches and cliffs on distant shores, exploring the desert wilds and deep forests, in a quest to find the place where you belong. The genealogy records have gaps, places where rotten teeth have been pulled, leaving empty sockets behind. It gnaws at you. Each time you are interrogated about your origins, you wonder: Where do you belong? How do you fit in? When you look in the mirror, the reflection is blank, and you are left with questions—nothing else.

You sign up to a registry and attempt to track your roots, but the evidence has been buried. Trace the genealogy backwards, and there it is: a thick line of ink scratched through the name of a lavender child who suddenly appeared in the family tree. No leaves. No branches. No roots. Just a handwritten denial of association written in the margins. Your family looks the other way when you ask too many questions. Your great-grandmother smiles and pats your hand. She tells you merfolk cannot cry, as if that makes the sorrow easier to bear. Finally, desperate to know the truth, you send a DNA kit to the lab.

The results only complicate things.

It begins like this:

Your skin is a different shade than anyone else in your family. When you ask about it, your parents tell you stories. Your relatives snigger as you walk into the room. Even though they speak in whispers, you can hear their comments, dark words spoken in dark corners. You don't belong and you know it. You are *other*. And, despite your many attempts to hide your *otherness*, everyone can see it.

Perhaps this is not your family, you think. Perhaps you are a changeling. When those explanations fail, you search deeper, always deeper. A close look at your skin under a lamp, under the sun, reveals the shimmer swimming in your veins. You've heard the whispers. Eager to claim your rights, you slice the skin and let your blood run free. It's only then you finally accept the truth. You are not the same as everyone else. You are alone.

And then it happens. You set out on a journey of self-discovery.

You've heard rumors of lost people who have searched for connections to the realms of faerie in wild woods. And then there are stories about others who wait, motionless in sand-swept deserts, hoping for truth to appear on the edge of an exhalation. You try the easiest ways first, the ones that leave your feet rooted to the ground. The deep green of ancient forests throbs with desire; the shifting deserts sing of solitude. Even so, those choices are no choices at all.

In your heart, you know you belong to the sea, and it belongs to you.

You continue your search on new shores. A jungle, thick and dark, tumbles down the slope. Made up of crushed bone and shell, the white sand powders your feet. The sea, a clear turquoise, beckons. You squint out over the water, but the only thing you see is a solitary seagull kiting on the breeze. You stand still, hoping to capture a fragment of harp song, but your kin remain silent, withdrawn.

Green children ghost into the shadows of the forest fringe. You stopped hiding behind hats and long sleeves years ago, and now the sun has deepened the lavender tint of your skin to the Tyrian purple extracted from crushed shells. The green children whisper back and forth in a language you cannot decipher. Their bare legs are covered with yellow mud. Spiked crowns of holly and black orchids rest on their small heads. High in the canopy a monkey howls. The green children retreat, disappearing back into the sheltering canopy, leaving you alone and unwanted on a foreign shore.

You head north, following the coast until the freezing seas deny further passage. At night, the northern lights dance in ribbons of red and green and blue. Sometime, a thread of lavender shines through in a beacon of hope before disappearing once more. The stars hum in a cloudless sky and moonlight skates across the fog, ice crystals suspended in the frigid air.

One arctic morning, you wake to find two crow girls watching you from their perch on the skeletal remains of a tree. Their eyes glitter like jet. In their hooded cloaks of black feathers, they are indistinguishable from one another. They point and chatter, a peppered exchange of gossip. Although you are certain you are a creature of the surf, you wonder what it would be like to belong to their flock. You take a step forward, arms outstretched, but the crow girls spook and take flight in a raucous spin of displaced snow.

You wish you could take solace in tears shed, but once again you are left to suffer without sound. Desperate, you search for threads of hope in your journal, but they crumble in colored bits of fragrance as you turn the page. When you head south for warmer climes, you leave your diaries and genealogy charts behind. And, after a while, you find contentment in the quiet of your solitude.

By this time, you've been travelling so long it's become a way of life—an ebb and flood of new scents and sounds. You've watched the intricate courtship dances of the nāga, their serpent tails coiling together in a rasping susurration. You've seen the silhouettes of the deer people swaying under the full moon in southwestern deserts. You've followed the immortals' rainbow dreams through the dry season.

When at last you land on the salty shore of a dead sea, the memories of unshed tears are truly lost. Even so, that nameless suffering lightens as you wander this desert on the far side of the world. No creature can survive in this scarred landscape, no fish or frog or fruit, yet you feel more alive than ever.

As you approach the vast stretch of the inland sea, plants laden with green globes dissolve in puffs of ash, leaving a trail of smoke in your wake. You seek access to the place where the water kisses the shore, a dead region littered with petrified driftwood and mineral deposits, but the path in uneven and broken. As you walk, the white sheets covering the earth crack and crumble under your feet like brittle bones returning to dust. You press on. And when you finally kneel to touch this dead sea, you are filled with the sense that you have finally come home.

From the point of contact where your fingers touch water, a kaleidoscope of concentric circles spreads out in rippled waves as far as you can see. The figure of a woman rises from the depths and glides towards you. She matches the landscape, an eerie combination of stark extremes. Her skin is the deep black of impenetrable shadow curled in the scattered remains of desiccated wood. Her hair billows behind her in a cloud of ash and smoke, and her eyes shine like black diamonds.

You stay on your knees and wait. As she edges closer, you can see the crystal deposits clinging to her skin, delicately arranged patterns that serve to magnify their nacreous brilliance. And in those arrangements, you finally find all the tears you've never shed. The sharp angles and panes of exquisite emotion revealed in tragic tears. The snowflake stars of gratitude fed by tributaries of hope. The city streets and dead ends contained in sorrow married to the cobbled asphalt of change. And the elegant reservoirs expressed in reunion.

In the woman's glittering eyes, you see the truth of your great-grandmother's words. The people of the sea have no tears, a price paid in pain. But now that you have found all those lost tears, generation upon generation of suffering deposited in a salty sea, you finally realize the truth; lavender children are never truly alone.

Just one step away, the keeper of the merfolk's tears reaches out to you. Worlds of weeping form, break apart, and reform in the cup of her outstretched palm. *Sorrow, joy, hope, change, tragedy.*

You take her hand in yours.

Reunion.

GREY MATTERS

As soon as she'd heard the news, Jenna put her dissertation on hold and caught the first flight heading north. Not that it did her any good. Her demands had been summarily dismissed by the grey-haired twins who'd commandeered the dissolution of the Chapman estate. Instead of granting her simple request, the old maids bumped her even further down the list. As she waited, Jenna consoled herself with the long violet-grey feather Birdie had mailed her just days before she'd died.

The unseasonable warmth promised an early spring, a promise echoed in the magnetic calls of geese migrating south. Jenna waited in the shade of a weeping willow near Chapman Pond. A great gaggle of geese churned like storm clouds along the path Birdie had worn down over decades from visits to these waters. Jenna mused on the times she'd followed her great-grandmother on that journey from the white house to the sanctuary where Birdie would spend hours talking with her geese. In return, each bird would pluck a precious wing feather or two, which her great-grandmother reverently bundled together before carrying them back to her room.

Jenna collected a clump of tattered down from the ground. She thought of Birdie and whispered a wish. The dirty white wisps floated from her palm and were swept away to ghost along the bleak shore.

By the time the grey twins called Jenna's name, the leftover casseroles had been put away and her relatives were comparing their spoils with increasingly sloppy toasts of rum punch. The two elderly women zealously guarded the front oak door. Angels armed with blazing swords couldn't have done a better job. Jenna didn't know much about fancy invitations or genealogy charts, but she was pretty sure the grey twins were technically great aunts of some sort or another and addressed them as such.

"Don't be ridiculous," said one of the women. "Birdie wasn't a true Chapman."

"Second wife," the other one added. They were indistinguishable from each other with their ashen skin and plain dresses. "No relation to us."

A flock of Canadian geese streamed overhead. As one, the grey women glared at the source of the noisy interruption until it had passed.

"Now then," said an aunt who was not an aunt, "you may choose one item and one item only from whatever's left in *that* woman's bedroom. Everything else belongs to the *real* Chapmans. Understand?"

"Yes." The other un-aunt agreed. "More than generous."

Jenna knew better than to argue. Birdie had told her that black and white were extremes and, like all extremes, they should be avoided as much as possible. In a way, this conviction shaped the way Jenna tried to portray the world through pigment and paint. Instead of stark contrasts, her art explored all the tints and shades in-between.

Jenna kept her head bowed, as she slipped past the grey women and rushed up the stairs to Birdie's bedroom. The door was wide open. Inside, the only remaining piece of furniture was the massive four-poster oak bedframe tagged with a claim by Elena Chapman-Dunst. Jenna remembered the childhood nights when she'd listened to Birdie's stories about winged women. It took all her effort to keep from crying when she realized the feathers scattered around the room had come from Birdie's duvet. Someone had ripped the fabric apart, rifled through those dreams, and then discarded them to drift into piles on the dusty floor.

Pressing back the urge to cry, Jenna settled on the bare mattress and listlessly sifted through the heap of scattered odds and ends. There was just one thing she really wanted. She could only cross her fingers it had been overlooked by all those cousins who weren't cousins and the aunts who weren't aunts. Jenna had almost given up hope, when she caught a glimpse of violet-grey peeking out from the down pushed into the corner.

Jenna combed through the fluff of discarded dreams to discover a bundle of stiff wing feathers held together with a frayed cord. She untied the knots and held her breath as she fanned the feathers open to reveal a cloak the color of cooled cinders and winter clouds.

Outside an open window, the geese called.

Jenna grinned and held the feathered cape close to her chest. Birdie's scent lingered on the fringe: a powdery dust of winter sunshine mixed with the grey-green promise of spring.

Eager to escape the hollow house, Jenna raced down the grand staircase. She dodged the grey women and dashed across the dying lawn to the shore of Birdie's pond. Geese shrouded the shore and spilled out on the dark water. The ones closest to her spread their wings and hissed a warning.

She looked over her shoulder at the stately, white-washed house where Birdie had spent the most precious moments of her youth. Birdie made her choice, but it wasn't the one Jenna wanted to claim for herself. The geese settled down when she whispered their names. She was meant to live a life painted in the many shades that existed between black and white. Jenna slipped the feathered cloak over her shoulders and spread her arms wide.

She was meant to fly.

FROM THREAD TO TEXTILE: A FLYING CARPET WEAVING MANUAL

Historical Note: While it's true that, once upon a time, the Queen of Sheba gifted King Solomon a magnificent green and gold silk rug as a sign of her favor, most of the flying carpets in this world keep their magic hidden in the weave of more mundane affairs. That most famous of magic carpets stretched sixty miles in length, a feat of woven wonder that took the combined effort of ten times ten masters more than ten years to complete. (After all, this was the Queen of Sheba making a romantic gesture meant to seduce a king into clandestine, moonlit affairs.) Even if the last of the crimson feathered, Sabaean dragons hadn't been killed by an overzealous knight in 1449, their silk would not be the preferred material today, as it loses some of its tensile strength when wet, and it can be weakened if exposed to too much sunlight. (In all reality, flying at night is highly over-rated. There's too much riffraff clogging up the air space. During the daylight hours, you can at least see what's coming.)

1. Shearing

If you are crafting a flying carpet these days, the best source for raw material can be found in the mountains of the legendary Caelum Isles. Guarded by a ruhk, a small flock of winged sheep roam the steep edges of the highest mountaintops. The fleece of these sheep shines with stardust, making them appear like shooting stars as they leap from peak to peak. But the true secret to their lustrous coats resides in a steady diet of the diamonds, rubies, and pearls growing in the rocky crags and crevices. Just keep in mind, the wool of a minimum of seven sheep is needed to create a carpet that will transport two people. (After all, what's the fun in flying alone?)

2. Carding

Once you've secured the coveted fleece of the winged sheep—unless you have access to King Sabut's fabled ebony horse, good luck with that—it's important to take the time to carefully card the wool, separating the fiber from the debris of everyday life in the Caelum Isles. After the fleece has been carefully scoured and carded, prepare the wool for hand spinning. Although spinning wheels come in handy for this time-consuming task, it's best to opt for a drop spindle and distaff, especially if you have any issues with fairy godmothers or angry djinn. In any case, hand spinning is almost mandatory as the stardust tends to jam modern machinery. (I never said it was going to be easy, now did I?)

3. Dyeing

There are many historians who believe that the power of a flying carpet exists in the dye used to color the fiber. (This continues to be debated, but it's probably in your best interest to support this belief.) In truth, there are several dyes which seem to increase the aerodynamics of magic carpets even though the proposed benefits of utilizing these dyestuffs haven't been substantiated by science. That being said, it is imperative to only use natural dyes in the construction of a flying carpet. Synthetic colors have been known to interfere with the performance of the fibers in the material plane. (It's never a good thing to have your equipment stall at 3,000 feet.)

Favored dyes found in fragments of ancient aerial textiles include dyer's rocket (*Reseda luteola*), which delivers a gorgeous yellow hue; the Asp of Jerusalem (*Isatis tinctoria*), which produces a fabulously rich indigo dye; and cochineal (*Dactylopius coccus*), the scales of which yields a scarlet pigment that brings new meaning to the word 'red.' You might think these hues are nothing new—after all, even Chaucer knew about them—but there's a trick in the gathering that has been held secret by elite weavers for thousands of years. For prime usage of these dyes in the construction of a flying carpet, the raw materials must be harvested on a blue moon and carefully steeped in a griffin's claw for forty days and forty nights. Only then should the dyes be added to the prepared fibers to settle in a copper pot. (Don't be in a hurry with this step. Trust me. It's worth the wait.)

4. Balling

Once you've brought the yarn to its preferred saturation of color—the brightest shades seem to work best, but be aware that these vibrant colors can also garner unwanted attention—dry the fibers in an airy, shadowed area. In all cases, it's best to keep the freshly dyed wool out of sight. Over the years, there have been a few accounts of a covetous simurgh stealing particularly beautiful skeins left in the open. (Some theories point to the creature's love of color as cause for the appropriation; others claim the response is related to beast's maternal nest building instincts.) After the drying is complete, roll the wool into balls of three-ply yarn to prepare the material for the weaving and knotting process.

5. Weaving

Once you have your full draft complete—the threading plan, the tie-up box, the treadling plan, and a draw-down of the weave structure—it's time to dress the loom. Despite what you may have heard, a flying carpet can be woven on either a vertical or a horizontal loom. The important part is that that the loom sits directly along the axis of a major ley line. (How else would you be able to combine the threads of energy into the web?) Each line of the textile must be woven by hand with thread delivered into the weft by a shuttle carved from a unicorn's horn. To finish, any knot can be used, but if you want to stick with the traditional route, I suggest the Turkish knot. This particular technique has the added benefit of providing another layer of protection as it invokes enchanted safeguards. (It isn't known for certain which enchantments this particular knot is connected to, but there haven't been any complaints so far. It *is* magic after all.)

6. Trimming

After the weaving is completed, remove the rug from the loom for the trimming process. This is when you should find a flat place where you won't mind spending hours upon hours smoothing the structure of the carpet by shearing off unnecessary fibers. (Diamond-edged scissors are the best for this intricate work.) Just keep in mind, this step can take several days, even for the most skillful of weavers. However, once the pile has been successfully trimmed, the patterns should be clear and the colors distinct in accordance with the original design.

7. Stretching

After trimming, the carpet should be washed with water from the Peirene spring. (You might even catch a glimpse of Pegasus while gathering the water needed; however, if instead you see the Muses gathered there, it's best to turn around and wait for another day. There is no reason to get involved in a philosophical discussion at this point in the process.) Once freshly washed, stretch the finished carpet on all sides and tie it to a frame to ensure its proper shape and size. After the sun has set over the horizon three times, your rug should be ready to be removed.

(You will know when it's time to untether your magic carpet as it will begin to vibrate against its constraints.)

8. Finishing

Despite all the preparation and work that goes into crafting a magic carpet, you will never really know if you've succeeded until your masterpiece takes its first flight. (Just to be safe, you might want to slowly test out your rug's abilities. Sometimes it can seem like these beauties have a mind of their own.) If for some reason your efforts failed, try not to be too torn up about it. (Creative arts can take time to perfect.) There is always next time and, if nothing else, you'll have at least created a beautiful conversation piece that can add a touch of elegance to just about any room of the house.

Happy flying!

A SEED PLANTED

The last time the portal opened, it did so high above the heads of millions of people going about their ordinary lives in an ordinary world. The media filled the networks with images and suppositions, but Kaliya disconnected the coverage with a decisive click. Despite what some people thought, it had happened before. She had read her father's reports. A ghost ship sailing through the sands of the Sahara Desert. Hanging gardens filled with vividly colored flowers floating down the Amazon River. Towers strung with enormous bells clamoring a strident alarm in the mountains of Nepal. However, unlike the most recent event, those sightings were easy to cover up with cleverly crafted stories.

"Optical illusions," the officials and scientists said, again and again. "Stacked spatial refractions. Atmospheric phenomenon related to thermal inversion. Mirage. Fata Morgana."

Kaliya knew better. The thin places between Earth and the shadow planet Ketu were expanding, stretched to a membrane no thicker than the sheen of a soap bubble rising through the air. Over the course of the latest three minute and thirty-three second event, a drift of golden seeds rained down from the sky. Before long, the tenuous borders between worlds would fail entirely. And Kaliya wasn't about to let that happen. She would make her father's dreams of sovereignty come true. She would be the one of his daughters to succeed where the others had failed. She would find the key to closing the portal to Ketu forever. And maybe, just maybe, he would forgive her, he would love her as he once had, the way he loved Beatrice still.

She tugged at the glove on her right hand, freeing each finger from its silken confines. Once she'd peeled the material away from her pale green skin, Kaliya pressed her hand against the access panel. It flashed purple, acknowledging her as one of Dr. Hawthorn's daughters. The door clicked open, and she removed her palm just as the panel began to pulse with a red warning light. A mist of antitoxins and sterilizers clouded the panel, obscuring the accusatory warnings. Kaliya scowled at the reminder and resheathed her hand, effectively creating a barrier between herself and anyone she might come in contact with.

The first time the portal to Ketu opened, at least for any scientifically measurable length of time that is, Kaliya's father had been a young man. There hadn't been any seeds drifting from a sky split in two, but the discovery of Ketu had inspired her father to engineer his greatest creations. Dr. Hawthorn had named his seven daughters after the mythical Indian *vishkanya*—damsels so poisonous they could kill with a kiss. He'd named the firstborn Beatrice, a mocking tribute to a dusty story written long ago. But Beatrice hadn't turned out as lethal as her literary counterpart. Dr. Hawthorn refined his experiments: Mara, Dakini, Camille, Jovelyn, Iolanthe, and, finally, Kaliya—the deadliest of them all.

Kaliya walked down the corridor leading to the inner sanctum. Unlike the rest of the compound's halls—crowded with apprentices rushing to fulfill their masters' whims—the Aconitum was nearly deserted. As usual, the filtered air and laboratory lighting left her feeling anxious and smothered. Sterile shelves of glass and steel lined both sides of the walkway. Relics from Ketu crowded the finely lit cases. Kaliya had spent her developmental years combing through the catalogues in search of clues on how to access the shadow world, but the relics had proved to be nothing more than fragments of a civilization just out of reach.

She paused for a moment in front of Caliburn, the legendary sword turned to stone. Although most of the granite was weathered to a dull grey, the hilt bore scars from more recent times. Kaliya could barely trace the echoes of the woman's face that had once graced the unearthly object. The memory of her father's hands grasping a chisel and hammer, forearms flecked with blood, however, was as bright as the metal he'd removed from her ribcage on her twelfth birthday. When Kaliya had recovered enough to return to the hall, she'd wept to discover Caliburn defaced. The stone shavings and the metal had disappeared, tucked away in one of her father's secret vaults, as though stone and bone had never existed. According to him, they never had.

At the end of the aisle, Kaliya moved through hermetically sealed doors from one ecosystem to another. Once inside, she breathed deep. The loamy smell of turned earth, the delicate scent of poisonous flowers, and the cloying sweetness of death was her heaven on earth. The entire biodome served as a greenhouse. Unlike the stale and sterile corridors leading to the heart of the Aconitum, the ceiling and sides of the central structure were constructed from reinforced glass. She sighed in relief and smiled.

In her youth, Kaliya and her sisters had roamed wild among the engineered plants. Up in the canopy of variegated leaves, Dakini's pale pink form could usually be found skipping and spinning along tree limbs that stretched across the artificial sky. But even Dakini's most graceful dances were just shadows when Camille was compelled to move. With her cinnamon skin and innate ability for martial arts, Camille was the first to realize her potential as a *vishkanya.* Jovelyn, with her love of sharp things, cultivated thorns as blue and as large as her hand, which she would whittle into makeshift knives. Their darker sister, Iolanthe, liked to keep her dusky violet skin damp. She could usually be found lurking the cunningly contrived springs and streams that wound through the biodome. Kaliya had loved them, and they had loved her. But that had all changed after the accident.

Kaliya gravitated to the fountain at the center of the dome. The sound of water frolicking among stone naiads always relaxed her. As she walked, she trailed her fingers along the curling vines that reached out to greet her. Near the fountain, her favorite flower bloomed. The air simmered with its deadly sweetness. Kaliya hummed a lullaby and tenderly gathered the dark purple blooms in her gloved hands.

"Good. You're here." Her father's voice rattled through protective filters.

Kaliya dropped her arms and turned to face him. His vivid blue eyes stared at her through the glass of his hazmat helmet. Kaliya could barely remember a time when she'd been able to touch him. And the last memory she *did* have was accompanied by tortured screams and blistered flesh.

"Hello Father." She peeled off her gloves and let them slip through her fingers to pool in coiled loops at the fountain's edge. "Is it time?"

He ignored her question and answered with one of his own. "You saw?"

Even though he was completely protected from accidental exposure, Dr. Hawthorn left a few steps untaken between them. Occupied by increasingly frequent appearances of the shadow planet and the threat it posed to his authority, he was more distant than ever.

That empty space reminded her of Beatrice, the first of them to be born. Unlike the others, Beatrice kept to herself, preferring the words of dead poets over the company of her sisters. Their father had protected his eldest daughter's desire for privacy, something denied to the rest of them. The only one of the sisters allowed near Beatrice was Mara, sweet as an overripe apricot and as lethal as the cyanide contained in its seed. Kaliya pretended she didn't care. But she had, and she'd tried everything she could to gain her father's favor. Kaliya had transformed herself into the perfect weapon, a weapon honed by hate and edged with envy. She just needed to prove she was better than Beatrice, better than them all.

"Yes." Kaliya leaned back against the stone, alert yet still taking advantage of the heat streaming through the glass dome. Let him come to her. "Do you have a sample?"

Her father frowned, but he closed the space between them and held out a sealed container. Inside, a scattering of seeds glittered, perfect golden ovals soaking up the sun. Kaliya reached out. She touched his hand, protected against biohazards, and paused. Her pale green skin appeared waxy and alive compared to the sterile white suit. He trembled, but he didn't pull away. The moment passed, and she collected the container. Kayila held it up and peered inside, marveling at the texture and color of the foreign seeds.

"They're beautiful," she said, awed by the potential she sensed.

"They're toxic," he snapped, "just like everything else that comes from that cursed planet."

Behind the faceplate, his lined face creased into even deeper furrows, and his lips pursued as though he'd sampled an especially bitter fruit. "The Watcher must have gone mad to release such destruction on Earth. She must be stopped."

As far as Kaliya could tell from her father's charts, the way between the two worlds had closed abruptly just months before Beatrice had been born. It had remained closed for more than three decades before suddenly appearing in the sky just a few months earlier.

Over the course of those long years, Dr. Hawthorn had secured a seat on the council and moved up in power through the judicious deployment of his daughters.

"The Watcher?" Kaliya traced the cockatrice etched into the clear lid.

Leave it to her father to take on the sigil of a creature that could kill with a glance. She still wasn't sure if it was his idea of a joke, or if it was a symbol of pride in the lethal daughters he'd managed to engineer out of sheer determination.

"There's a balance that must be maintained." Dr. Hawthorn looked up as though he could see through the dome, past the city's protective shield, and through the brane that separated Earth from her shadow sister, Ketu.

Kaliya followed his gaze. The only thing she saw was the network of branches criss-crossing the dome like a neural network programmed to feed the fancies of a daredevil dancer. But there was no promise of pink among the green. Daniki had been one of the first of Dr. Hawthorn's daughters to leave the Aconitum on assignment. She never returned.

Kaliya twisted the lid off the container and lifted a single seed to her lips. She ran her tongue over its smooth surface, feeling the contours, tasting its potential, before swallowing it whole. She repeated the process two more times and then recapped the container, handing it back to her father. "Do you have the coordinates and times pinned down for the next event?"

"I'm a scientist, not a spy." Dr. Hawthorn frowned through the faceplate. "The Harp must be silenced. The portal to Ketu must be closed forever, or everything I've built will be destroyed. Do you understand?"

"Yes, Father." She looked through the glass, hoping to catch a glimpse of pride in those blue eyes.

His expression remained calm and clinical, as though he was comparing her to someone else and found her lacking.

"Don't fail me this time."

"Father." Kaliya looked away and gathered her gloves from their resting place on the fountain's edge.

***

Although she knew the basic whereabouts of the place where Beatrice had taken refuge from the outside world, she'd never been there. Yet, after an hour of wandering the winding garden paths, she found her eldest sibling puttering away in the rose beds as though she were a common gardener.

"Hello Beatrice."

Her sister froze, pale yellow hands sunk deep in the loamy soil. Of all of Dr. Hawthorn's daughters, Beatrice was the loveliest. She matched the billowy blooms of the hybrid rose she tended. The golden glow of the Alchymist mirrored Beatrice's creamy yellow skin and unbound apricot hair. Her sister's tensed shoulders released, and she returned to her work as though a visit from her deadliest sibling was a welcome event.

The history between the sisters said otherwise.

All of Dr. Hawthorn's *vishkanya* had kills to their credit by the time they reached puberty, all of them except his beloved Beatrice. After the accident, he'd married off his most precious flower to a close ally, the one man on Earth who'd managed to chart the stars of the dark universe that existed alongside their own.

Kaliya was the only one of the sisters who had not been invited to the wedding.

The dark green leaves of the climbing roses stretched up to soak in the sun, but the flowers shifted to follow the face of the poet who tended them. The perfume of Beatrice's fear lay heavy in the air.

"I never understood your fascination with roses," Kaliya said, as she moved to kneel next to her sister. "But this strain is lovely in its own way, I suppose."

Kaliya peeled off her gloves and stroked the variegated petals. Her thumb smudged the colors into a wilted blend as the plant struggled under her touch. Out of the corner of her eye, she saw her sister's peach-colored lips tremble.

"What do you want?"

Kaliya plucked a petal from its stem and lifted it to her mouth. She brushed the creamy velvet against her lips. Its heavy scent was filled with notes of liquid sunshine and honeyed musk. The damp decay of the turned soil tempted the golden seeds lodged in her throat. She suppressed the desire to give them life. Not yet.

"You've been gone a long time, sister." Kaliya placed the rose petal on her tongue and carefully crushed its delicate beauty between her teeth. "You're not his favorite anymore."

Beatrice looked at her then. Her eyes were the same vivid blue as their father's. "I was never his favorite."

"You were his first." Kaliya plucked another petal from the rose and popped it in her mouth. Its softness only sharpened her hunger. "He protected you."

"I might have been the first of us to be born, but you are his last hope."

Kaliya moved closer. "What do you mean?"

Beatrice appeared to wilt before her. Unlike Kaliya, Beatrice had been created for beauty. Her only claim to being one of Dr. Hawthorn's *vishkanya* was in the subtle effects she had on men's desire. Her poison had a light touch; it thinned the blood, made the heart race. Beatrice had no resistance to her youngest sister's deadly nature. The faded scars on her arms proved it.

"There is a story about Father," Beatrice said, appearing calm despite the surge of fear perfuming her pores. "They say he found a way to Ketu, that he stole riches from the ruler."

"Everyone knows that." Kaliya reached out and trailed a finger across her sister's dirt-covered knuckles. Beatrice flinched, but didn't scream, not even when her skin began to darken to a dirty gold.

"They are evil creatures, those who live in the shadow world," Kaliya continued. "They must be stopped."

"There is evil in both worlds." Beatrice took a deep breath as her skin smoldered under the press of Kaliya's fingers. "Iolanthe is dead."

The golden seeds rooted in Kaliya's throat twisted at the sound of her favorite sister's name. Iolanthe had been the last of the sisters sent away, leaving Kaliya alone with their father in the Aconitum. The cloying taste of violets flooded her mouth. "You don't know that."

"Yes," she said. "I do."

Beatrice turned to fully face her sister, knee to knee, nose to nose. "Listen to me, Kaliya. Our father stole more than gold from Ketu." She grasped her sister's hands, creamy yellow enfolding pale green. "He stole us. He stole the golden eggs from which we were born." Kaliya tried to pull away as Beatrice's subtle hues blackened under her deadly touch. "And then he turned us into weapons."

"That's not true," Kaliya said. "He created us to save the world, but you thought you were better than everyone else. You left us there even though you knew what he was doing to us."

Beatrice shook her head even as she continued to fade like a photograph left too long in the sun. The resemblance to their aging, blue-eyed father made her look almost human.

Kaliya's voice rose, and her grip tightened. "He cut my ribs out and you didn't stop him. You could have at least *tried*."

"I'm sorry." Beatrice leaned forward and pressed a kiss on Kaliya's dark green lips. "You're the only one strong enough to defeat them both." Her breath stuttered. "That's why he saved you for last."

Her last words whispered their way past a swollen tongue.

"Both? What do you mean?"

Beatrice's lifeless hands fell free, and she slumped into the bed of roses she'd been so lovingly tending. Her apricot-colored hair turned brittle, and her skin lost its lustrous sheen—a dead rose resting in a thicket of thorns. Kaliya pressed her fingers to her lips, where the scent of crushed roses lingered.

***

Kaliya left her Beatrice lying in the dirt and made her way into her brother-in-law's study. She sorted through the classified files, following the trail from one source document to another, until she was finally able to narrow down the most probable location for the next event.

It seemed unlikely that it would occur so close to the last sighting, but the seeds she'd swallowed confirmed the direction she needed to go. She could feel their potential spiraling through her veins. The seeds acknowledged her as one of their own, a safe place to hide until they were needed. They would take her to the ruler in the sky, the king who had once wielded Caliburn in its true form. She had questions only he could answer.

And then she would kill him with a kiss one hundred times deadlier than any toxin known to man. After all, she'd been created for the sole purpose of assassination. And the conqueror living in that floating fairy castle was her first priority. And after that, acquisition of the fabled Harp and the destruction of the Watcher.

By the time Kaliya reached her destination, the golden seeds had taken root deep in her chest. With each breath, they pumped their toxic mix into her bloodstream. She felt different, alive, and more powerful than ever.

She glanced up, gauging the reach of the coalescing clouds. The towering formation was identical to the one photographed during the last event. Crops stretched out in ploughed symmetry around her. Kaliya breathed deep, searching for kinship to the land, but underneath the scent of growth she detected the stench of chemicals designed to kill.

Kaliya bent at the waist and began to cough, a harsh and brutal sound that intruded on the deathly silence surrounding her. The three seeds released their hold, working their way up her throat until she was able to spit them into a cupped palm. The sunlight broke through the clouds and shone down to illuminate the golden orbs she cradled so tenderly. She crouched and scooped out a hollow in the fertile soil where she deposited her charges.

And then she began to sing.

After just a few bars, the vines broke through the thin crust. They twined around each other as they thickened and lengthened, climbing towards the clouds. When they reached a height and breadth sturdy enough to bear her weight, Kaliya embraced the braided ropes and let them lift her skywards. The burnt sugar smell of violets exploded into the air as tiny purple flowers budded and opened along the green length of the vine. *Iolanthe.*

Kaliya continued to sing. The haunting melody reached deep into the material plane, plucking the strings that pulled the worlds together. She sang about the green and the sun and the water. She sang about disease and darkness and death. She sang about hope and despair. She sang a lament for her six dead sisters, flowers bloomed and buried before their time. And just as the vines broke through the clouds, the portal to Ketu opened. Through that window, a city from the shadow world came into view.

Kaliya's breath caught in her throat. The notes stumbled and then fell into silence. The rip in the sky spread until it came to a halt, just a step away from where she clung to the towering vines. The previous event had lasted just a few minutes, but there was no guarantee this portal would remain open as long. Kaliya looked down at the fields spread out below and wondered if she'd ever return. She had no reinforcements, no back-up plan, no escape route. But she couldn't go back, not now. She released her hold on the vines. And jumped.

Her feet landed on solid ground, but a part of her was surprised it wasn't just another mirage, that she didn't plummet through the clouds to the fields she'd left behind. Thick mist coiled around her legs. Dark shapes hunched in the shadows. She paused and rocked back on her heels, preparing for an attack. Nothing moved.

Sunlight broke through a seam in the clouds, revealing the stone precipice where she'd landed. Directly ahead of her, a watchtower blocked the path to the city beyond. Beneath the retreating wisps of fog, the bleak landscape revealed rocks blackened and scorched by flame. The green part of her shied away from the desolation, but the part of her trained to kill shrugged and moved forward, intent on completing her mission, whatever the cost.

Kaliya approached the watchtower. The silence of the lonely landscape pricked at her exposed skin. A feeling of *wrongness* settled deep in her chest, but there was nothing to fear in this dead land. No birds winged across the open sky. No animals thrived in the barren stretch. The attack on the watchtower had wreaked complete devastation.

A violent staccato of harp strings startled her. In response, the sky darkened and the ground shuddered, nearly throwing Kaliya to her knees. She grasped a boulder to brace herself. The darkness retreated, the ground stilled, and the door between worlds closed once more. Kaliya's palm came away from the rock smudged with soot. She lifted her hand and sniffed, catching a hint of perfumed violets beneath the smoke.

"I wouldn't do that, if I were you," said a musical voice.

Kaliya straightened, briskly rubbing her hands across her thighs. She turned to face the threat.

A woman stepped from a shadowed doorway set in the stone tower. She wore a cloak the color of amethyst. It shaded her face and flowed from her shoulders like a jewel turned liquid. She pushed back the cloak's hood and stared at Kaliya across the blackened waste.

If she hadn't seen her move, Kaliya would have thought the woman to be a cleverly constructed metal sculpture. Her skin held the sheen of polished bronze, her eyes were plated with gold foil, and her hair hung down in a sheet of quicksilver.

Kaliya flexed her fingers. "Who are you?"

The woman sighed through copper lips, a lovely rush of breath that sounded like chimes spinning in the breeze. "Your sisters didn't know me either, but I did hope it would be different with you."

"My sisters?" Kaliya edged closer as she assessed her enemy.

"They were all lovely in their own ways," said the bronze woman. "You father was quite inventive."

"What do you know about my father?"

Up close, she realized the bronze woman's cloak didn't just appear to be moving. It was composed of hundreds of butterflies, which were slowly opening and closing their iridescent wings. When fanned open, the insect's wings revealed shimmery scales painted in every imaginable hue of purple and indigo.

"I know more about Jack Hawthorn than you might expect," she replied with a frown. Her golden eyes flashed in the sun.

Kaliya sorted through memories of Ketu's relics and the catalogue of hints she'd gleaned over the years. She didn't like the direction the thoughts were taking her.

"Surely you can see. Your world is diseased, and that contamination is spreading." The bronze woman cast a glance out across the blackened landscape. "That is not an acceptable option."

"Where is Iolanthe?" Kaliya edged closer. The bronze woman's scent carried the tang of mineral oil. Other fragrances drifted to Kaliya from the wings of the butterflies: the decadence of damask rose, the dripping sweetness of jasmine, the velvety bite of snapdragons, the languid seduction of magnolia, the exotic musk of ylang-ylang, the cloying burn of violet. "Where is my sister?"

"Jack stole many treasures on the occasions he was here, but his last theft was unforgiveable." The bronze woman appeared lost in thought: the metallic veneer of her features made it difficult to read her emotions.

One of the amethyst butterflies disengaged from the cloak and fluttered over to land on Kaliya's arm. With its wings spread wide, the butterfly was as large as an open hand. The velvety softness of its indigo body rivaled the petals of even the most delicate of flowers. Kaliya waited for the insect to shrivel up and die. Instead, it tasted her skin with golden feet. The creature's slender purple antenna waved excitedly, and it began to make a clicking sound, which was picked up by the other butterflies clinging to the bronze woman's back.

The bronze woman returned her attention to Kaliya. “I have something to show you.”

Intrigued, Kaliya acquiesced with a curt nod. After all, her father had never said anything about a woman made from living metal.

Kaliya followed her into the watchtower.

Together, they climbed a long swirl of stairs that spiraled along the tower’s curving walls. They walked in silence, each step bringing them closer to the top. There were no doors, no windows. However, ghostly blue flames burned in globes hung from hooks set in the walls at evenly spaced intervals. The illumination from each globe only reached as far as the halo cast by the next light. In between, shadows prowled. There was no guardrail to protect against the deepening hollow in the center of the tower, nothing to keep someone from falling. Or being pushed. The stone steps encircled the dark emptiness, giving the illusion of a pit that plummeted down forever.

As they climbed, Kaliya thought about her sisters, the poisonous garden curated by their father. She thought about the games they’d played growing up and the more violent competitions as their individual assets developed. They had been fierce and beautiful and deadly. The list of kills confirmed it. *No more*, she reminded herself. She was the last of their kind. If she failed on this mission, if she failed to return, her father would be left alone.

What then? Would Dr. Hawthorn make more daughters to discard on the wings of a whim? *If so*, she thought, *why hadn’t he made them already?*

When it seemed as though they would continue to climb forever, the stairs suddenly stopped in front of a door painted the darkest shade of blue. The bronze woman glanced over her shoulder.

“Just try to remember I’m only offering you the truth.” She pushed the door open. “Nothing more.”

A golden light illuminated the top of the tower. Open windows stretched from floor to ceiling, and an aperture cut in the dome above directed a spotlight of sun on a round table in the center of the room. The table was inlaid with lapis lazuli and trimmed with gold, but the opulent design was overshadowed by the contents of the crystal case it supported.

Inside the case, golden eggs nestled in folds of purple satin. Each egg, cradled in a nest of silver vines, was the size of a man’s fist. Seven of those nests were empty, the silver vines tarnished black, the purple swaddling missing. In the others, the purple satin rustled as if in response to their entrance. *Butterflies*, she thought. *Not satin.*

The bronze woman laid a gentle hand on Kaliya’s arm. “He couldn’t carry any more than that.”

Although made of metal, her hand was as warm and supple as living flesh. The woman did not blacken and die from the exposure to Kaliya's skin. If anything, it shone a little brighter. Kaliya looked up from the bronze woman's hand, to stare at those seven empty cradles. Seven eggs stolen. Seven sisters with skin the color of flowers and sweat the sweetest of deadly perfumes. In the space from one second to another, all the little deceptions and clever clues clicked into place.

"Where is the Harp?" The butterfly perched on Kaliya's forearm began to croon and she absentmindedly stroked its velvety wings. "What does he want it for?"

The bronze woman opened the folds of her living cloak to expose her body. The metallic skin ended along the ridge of her collarbone, leaving the woman's rib cage exposed. The bones curved away from a silver spine, and strung between those gleaming branches, golden strings quivered.

"I am the Harp, my sweet girl." The bronze woman plucked the thinnest string. The clear note reverberated off the stone walls and the ground rumbled in response. "I open the door."

Kaliya dropped her hand. "Who are you?"

The bronze woman laughed, a tinkling of silver bells.

Kaliya stepped away, moving closer to the crystal case and its treasure. "Are all the people in Ketu like you?"

The bronze woman's smile turned sharp. "There is no one like me."

"What do you want?" Kaliya approached the case.

"Don't be such a child," said the bronze woman. "Your father didn't send you here to kill me. I can't be killed. I am eternal."

"You're the one who let him in, aren't you?"

The bronze woman shrugged. The butterflies dropped away in a swirl of velvet wings and perfumed flight.

Kaliya looked out a window cut into the stone wall. Outside the tower, the blackened landscape stretched on for miles before disappearing into the grey softness of clouds blooming with the promise of snow. There were no trees for Dakini to dance in, no warriors for Camille to fight, no springs for Iolanthe to haunt. She had a feeling that there was no one left to sail ships on the seas of Ketu. No flowers bloomed in the hanging gardens. And the bells had been silenced in the empty towers of the shadow world's capitol.

"You're the Watcher, aren't you?"

The bronze woman pivoted on a heel and waltzed to the table. "I love round things," she said as she ran her finger along the table's gilt edge.

Round things. Kaliya centered her thoughts, keeping her enemy close while she sorted through a dizzying array of images—the woman's face engraved in the stone sword, bronze bones removed and replaced, the cunning glimmer in her father's eyes. She could almost taste the golden seeds that had rained down from a broken sky. "Was it always you?"

The bronze woman smiled again. "Of course."

Dr. Hawthorn's *vishkanya* carried his code in their DNA, some more than others. But the potential she and her sisters embodied came from somewhere else. It came from *someone* else.

The clouds rolled closer.

"Is there anything alive left in this place?"

"Ketu has been purified." Those flat golden eyes narrowed; her copper lips curled. "Earth is next."

Kaliya closed the space between them. The bronze woman watched her, wary.

"Who did this to you, Mother?"

"He lied to me," she said. "He's a deceiver."

"Yes." At this distance, the enormity of her father's manipulations was something to behold. "He lied to us all."

The bronze woman tilted her head as though listening to a tune being played far in the distance. "There's a storm coming," she said, her voice hollow.

Kaliya took three long steps, closing the space between them. "Everything will be fine, Mother. I know what to do."

She reached out to embrace the bronze woman. Kaliya wondered how different her life and the lives of her sisters would have been without their father's machinations. Might Ketu still be a thriving world filled with the color and beauty promised in those broken relics displayed on sterile shelves? Had there ever been an alternative timeline where she could have thrived under gentle guidance and a mother's touch? Were the *vishkanya*, living experiments stolen from the shadow planet, destroyers or saviors? Kaliya thought it depended on the point of view.

"Look what he has done to you, my pretty girl." The bronze woman stroked Kaliya's cheek with fingers so warm they almost burned. "He's made you a monster."

"I know, Mother."

Kaliya tightened her embrace, the golden Harp pressed hard against her. She spread her legs, rooted her feet, and began to hum. Her body responded. Leafy tendrils sprouted from her skin. Her toes lengthened and stretched deep into the stone, breaking it apart as she settled her weight. Her fingers latched together, elongating and vining into a tangle of branches binding the bronze woman. And then, she lifted the smallest finger on her left hand and concentrated: the nail elongated and sharpened to thin point. Kaliya slipped it beneath the gold foil of her mother's eye and pierced the rotting remains of her brain. The bronze woman went still in her daughter's embrace.

Kaliya's song deepened. The butterflies guarding their golden charges joined in the song. Kaliya thought of her sisters as she sang. She thought of Beatrice and her delicate hothouse beauty. She thought of Mara's love of sweets and Dakini's desire to dance. She thought of Camille's passion for women and Jovelyn's penchant for knife play. And she thought of Iolanthe trailing the burnt scent of violets as she cut though her opponents with her razor wit.

The loud crash of stone falling away from the sides of the tower competed with the clamor of dozens of golden shells being torn apart by their occupants. Each crack in the eggs was accompanied with the trill of pure notes slicing through the golden shells. Some of the butterflies pulled the shards away with their delicate feet. Others flew in a dizzying spiral around Kaliya, but still she continued. Her vines tore away the sides of the stone tower, allowing the light from Ketu to shine freely in the room. She shattered the crystal case, freeing her new siblings from their cages.

Finally, when the last of the tower walls had been torn down and the remnants of the golden shells crumbled to a dust of glittering fragments. Kaliya tossed her hair behind the curving bark spread across her shoulders. *A gift for you too, Father.*

The dark strands of hair shifted into a delicate filigree of stems. At the end of each strand, dark purple flowers sprouted. A breeze lifted the strands to release the deadly perfume of delicate blooms. Under her guidance the flowers turned to seed, which separated and lifted into the sky. The churning clouds curled around the tower's base would carry the seeds to Earth, where her progeny would flourish.

As the seeds floated free, Kaliya took a moment to marvel at the beauty of her younger siblings, a new generation hatched to bring life back to Ketu. She would keep them safe. She would stand watch. Their enemies would never be allowed to harm them. All the humans would be strangled by a kiss one hundred times deadlier than any toxin known to man. And the Earth would thrive in the green places. At her touch, the golden Harp strings thrummed.

And the door opened.

AFTERWORD

In June 2013, I walked into the social security office to pick up one of the last pieces of paper I needed to create a new identity. I am one of the lucky ones. I am a domestic violence survivor, but my bid for safety came at a high price. Everything linked to my birth name and original social security number was wiped away: my entire work history, a fifteen-year career as a freelance journalist, four college degrees, several professional certifications, government clearance, and more.

However, there was a silver lining. I finally had the opportunity to pursue a career in fiction, something I hadn't been able to balance with the workload I carried in my old life.

And so, I emerged quietly. My first publication as Carina Bissett was the poem "Wild Girl," which was published in the first issue of *NonBinary Review*. I will always be grateful to Zoetic Press publisher and editor-in-chief Lise Quintana for nurturing my work in those early years.

To my surprise, I was still alive in 2016. My abuser had not found me, and so I stretched a little more and applied to the University of Southern Maine for the MFA creative writing program at Stonecoast. When I was accepted, I was certain I was finally on the way to fulfilling my dreams.

I should have known better.

Three weeks before my first writing residency, I was in a freak bicycle accident. I was knocked unconscious and woke up eighteen hours later with multiple contusions and a traumatic brain injury (TBI). I realize now that I should have delayed my participation at Stonecoast, but I was terrified this opportunity would slip through my fingers. Two weeks after being released from the hospital, I limped onto a plane with a bag full of medications. This was not my best decision.

Needless to say, I realized I was in trouble when the director of the program staged an intervention halfway through my first residency. I'd completed my readings before the accident, but the cognitive impairment from the TBI meant I couldn't process new material. And I was unable to write a coherent sentence, let alone an entire story.

The day after I returned from that first residency, I had the second of four facial reconstructions. I also had two additional knee surgeries. But somehow, I survived. And then, I began to write.

At the end of 2016, the interactions I was having with a writer on Facebook changed my life. I don't remember the exact day I met Dr. Angela Slatter online, but I do remember that she was one of the first people to truly take my fiction seriously. She gave me feedback and, in doing so, taught me how to write. But more than that, she showed me kindness during the darkest point in my life. I will always be grateful for all the lessons I've learned from her, and there are more than I can count.

As I write this afterword, it's been ten years to the month since I walked into that social security office to complete my new identity as Carina Bissett. Today, I am married to a wonderful man who has taught me how to trust again. I have a safe space to pursue my dreams. And I am surrounded by a community of truly brilliant writers. There was a time when I thought I'd never see the day when my name appeared on the cover of a short story collection. But here it is, and I'm grateful to everyone who lifted me up along the way. Thank you for making my dreams come true.

PUBLICATION HISTORY

DEAD GIRL, DRIVING first published in *What Remains*, Firbolg Publishing, May 2022.

THE STAGES OF MONSTER GRIEF: A GUIDE FOR MIDDLE-AGED VAMPIRES first published in *Coffin Blossoms,* Jolly Horror Press, October 2020.

TWICE IN THE TELLING first published in *Upon a Twice Time*, Air and Nothingness Press, May 2021.

GAZE WITH UNDIMMED EYES AND THE WORLD DROPS DEAD first published in *Terror at 5280',* Denver Horror Collective, November 2019.

CRACKED first published in *Stonecoast Review*, Issue #9, July 2018.

AN EMBRACE OF POISONOUS INTENT first published in *Bitter Distillations,* Egaeus Press, December 2020.

THE CERTAINTY OF SILENCE first published in *Twisted Anatomy*, Sci-Fi & Scary, February 2021.

ROTTEN first published in *Arterial Bloom*, Crystal Lake Publishing, April 2020.

BURNING BRIGHT first published in *Gorgon: Stories of Emergence,* Pantheon, February 2019.

THE GRAVITY OF GRACE original to this collection.

MORE WINGS THAN THE WIND KNOWS first published in *Perseus & Medusa*, Issue #4, *Timeless Tales,* June 2015.

SERPENTS AND TOADS first published in *Enchanted Conversations*, April 2017.

AN AUTHENTIC EXPERIENCE first published in *WILD: Uncivilized Tales from Rocky Mountain Fiction Writers,* RMFW Press, *August 2020.*

WATER LIKE BROKEN GLASS first published in *Into the Wood*, Black Spot Books, November 2022.

THE FIRST DAY OF THE WEEK first published in *Flash Fiction Online*, November 2023.

AVIATRIX UNBOUND first published in *Triangulation: Extinction*, August 2020.

THE LANDSCAPE OF LACRIMATION first published in *The Hunger*, May 2018.

GREY MATTERS first published in *Chrysalis: Fairy Tale Transformations*, Fantasia Divinity Magazine, February 2020.

FROM THREAD TO TEXTILE: A FLYING CARPET WEAVING MANUAL original to this collection.

A SEED PLANTED first published in *Hath No Fury,* Ragnarok Publications, August 2018.

ACKNOWLEDGEMENTS

Putting together a collection can be a terrifying experience. Without Dr. Angela Slatter this book would not exist. I am grateful for her confidence in my work and her guidance on this journey.

I'd also like to thank the other mentors and teachers in my life, especially Richard Thomas, Elizabeth Hand, Nancy Holder, Cate Marvin, and Cara Hoffman. You have helped me become a better writer as well as a better person.

Thank you, Julie C. Day for writing the introduction to this collection, as well as for all the books we've created together and all those yet to come.

Thank you to my many beta readers and friends, including KT Wagner, Roni Stinger, Dr. Nike Sulway, Chip Houser, Daniela Tomova, Hillary Dodge, Priya Sharma, Steve Toase, Sarah Read, Gio Clairval, Kathrin Köhler, Marianne Kirby, Karen Bovenmyer (née Karen Menzel), Claire Eliza Bartlett, Sita Romero, Mark Bailen, Brian D. Hinson, Alison Colwell, and Lena F.

When my computer died, my friend Chris Seggerman and his lovely wife Krista Long contributed funds along with my wonderful father to make certain that I was able to buy a new one. I also want to thank every writer who took a workshop with me at The Storied Imaginarium over the last seven years. You continue to inspire me.

I'm eternally grateful to Scarlett R. Algee and the team at Trepidatio Publishing for giving this collection a home.

And thank you to Richard Lorenzen, my husband, for reading every word I write and for believing in me even when I'd given up hope. This book is for you.

ABOUT THE AUTHOR

Carina Bissett is a writer and poet working primarily in the fields of dark fiction and fabulism. Her work has been published in numerous journals and anthologies including *Into the Forest: Tales of the Baba Yaga*, *Upon a Twice Time, Bitter Distillations: An Anthology of Poisonous Tales*, and *Arterial Bloom*. Her poetry has been nominated for the Pushcart Prize and the Sundress Publications Best of the Net and can be found in the *HWA Poetry Showcase*, *Fantasy Magazine*, and *NonBinary Review*. She is also the co-editor of the award-winning anthology *Shadow Atlas: Dark Landscapes of the Americas*. Links to her work can be found at http://carinabissett.com.

Printed in the USA
CPSIA information can be obtained
at www.ICGtesting.com
JSHW020809210324
59608JS00006B/30